Other books by Michael Mood

WHISTLER'S ANGEL

Worldbreaker: Book 1

Michael Mood
©2017

For Jenna

⛤ **PART 1: AIR** ⛤

△ CHAPTER 1 △

The wind was clawing at Whistler's nostrils, like a cat begging to be let in before a storm.

The air had more than just a scent, he suddenly realized. It had a completeness of sensation; an emotion that gripped him by the shoulders, shook him, refused to let go.

As the wind shifted direction, Whistler felt it begin to *hunt*. It parted the grasses in the fields as if it might uncover a secret. It ran its long, powerful fingers through the thin stalks, pushing and kneading and bending, forcing the prairie to bow to its invisible will.

It felt like something bad was brewing.

The sky didn't look menacing, though. Whistler squinted up at it from under the wide brim of his straw hat. The wind had dried his eyes a bit and the sun was blistering overhead. He could see no signs of tornado in any direction. There was barely a cloud. Nothing remarkable about the weather.

Except the wind.

Whistler dropped the scythe from his shoulder and resumed swinging it, content to believe that his imagination had been riled by tedium.

Slish.

Slish.

Slish.

The best scything was before the sun was up and the grass still had its moisture, but Whistler had been up late the night before, sitting alone in his modest farmhouse and drinking immodest amounts of moonshine. He had barely made it to the barn in time to alleviate the cow of her milk supply.

Do things as you have time, Whistler, he thought.
*It's not the end of the world. No. No, that happened three
years ago.*

The grass piled up on his left side as he moved
forward, slowly and methodically cutting the field. Try to
take on too much grass at once and the scythe wouldn't cut,
walk too crooked a path and efficiency would be lost.
Patience. Steadiness. The grass fell before him, patches of
delicious clover mixed in periodically. The sureness of this
repetitive and familiar chore helped settle his mind again.
For a moment he grabbed hold of a feeling: the one that
says 'I can do anything. I am one man against the whole
world, and I can win.' Then that feeling was gone, the wisps
of it draining away like so many happy memories.

And onward the wind searched.

Whistler's three horses pranced in the field to the
west. They stayed nobly within the boundaries of the
ignoble fencing that contained them: wooden posts and
wooden boards all in disrepair. It would hold them for
another half a year, but not much longer. It was probably
time to remake it; not just to mend the holes, but to rebuild
the entire fence.

*I don't have time for everything I need to do. Have
I ever?*

Whistler walked and cut, the ground smooth and
even under the raspy soles of his dilapidated boots. There
was no one around to take care of his footwear but himself,
and he was no leather worker. So rain would get in, and
dust would get in, and the cracked leather would sometimes
flake off, but on he walked.

On he shuffled.

My legs don't work as well as I remember, he
thought.

But that thought made him worry: maybe it wasn't

his legs that were defective, but his memory.

Nah, it's not my mind. It's my legs for sure.

Flexibility had never been Whistler's forte, but lately he had been feeling more and more like a man made of metal, wanting to bend more fully than he was capable of. It was like yearning to take a full breath and not being able to.

From my father's blood, he thought.

The old man had been built like a draft horse, with limbs like clubs and a body like a barrel. But where that build had worked for his father, Whistler had never truly settled into it. He had never felt quite at home in his own skin. To say that Whistler was powerful wouldn't have been a lie, but to say that he was well-constructed might have been.

His fingers had always been rather dumb. Normal-sized pockets had always been difficult for him to get things in and out of. Working with small objects always proved too infuriating. He had given up learning to write at an early age, not because his mind couldn't handle it, but because his fingers simply refused.

Slish.

Slish.

Slish, the scythe swung.

The world had a language of its own, beyond the written word, and Whistler had learned it and forgotten it over and over again. More times than he could remember. When his body and mind were silent the world spoke to him, filling in the gaps with its chaotic language. The lows of cattle. The crunch of the soil. The scars of a prairie fire. The hush of night. The twitter of a bird. The scent of the air before, during, and after a storm.

And right now the wind.

He shouldered his scythe and listened again.

"What are you sayin'?" he said slowly. "Somethin' . .
."

He concentrated.

He heard a melody, then, as he listened. He tried to focus on it, and it almost eluded him, but he caught it with a deft ear. It wasn't random. It repeated, over and over. He had to filter out all the other murmurings of the world and really *listen*, but there it was. The strangeness of today's wind wasn't in its chaos, but rather its order.

Whistler (who hadn't earned his nickname by happenstance) brought his lips together and joined in with the melody he was hearing. There were ten distinct tones in a repeating order. The melody flowed from his mouth, a higher-pitched twin of the wind's own.

One time through.

He lost himself in thought. His eyes glazed over, felt numb. The notes flew from his lips as the world seemed to slow around him. His scythe drifted from his hands and hit the ground with a dull thud.

Two times through.

He wouldn't have known his name if you had asked him. But in the absence of thought, memories came flooding back. Ones he had tried to keep out. He remembered *her*. He'd tried not to think about her for three years now, but of course that had been impossible. Three years wasted. Alone. Empty. So empty. He kept whistling.

On the third time through the melody something happened.

△

Whistler broke from his trance with a shudder that ran through his massive body. He reacted out of instinct, backpedaling just in time as a radiant *something* streaked to the ground, colliding with the earth where he had just been standing.

Whistler shielded his eyes with his hand, unable to open them even a crack despite that thick barrier. The light crept around the edges of Whistler's flesh, across the brim of his hat, and through his eyelids. He was forced to turn away as his head filled with pain.

The fallen thing was to Whistler's back now and he saw the luminous beams extending past him, his own body making a human-shaped disruption in the otherwise solid wall of light. Slowly it faded, but Whistler was still frightened to turn around, or really to move at all. So he waited, not trusting his senses, trying to decide if he was on fire or not.

Whistler had never been good in emergencies. His brain was deep and vast; not a series of puddles, but an ocean. He needed to work information thoroughly, like a cow chewing its cud. It never did anyone any good to mistake him for unintelligent, but it was accurate to say that he was slow.

Either the light was fading now or Whistler was slowly being blinded by it.

No, not blinded.

He could see the barrier of trees that outlined his property off in the distance. He looked at his hands and could see them, large and flat and calloused.

Satisfied with his diagnosis that the light was fading he turned around slowly. The thing that had fallen lay on the ground. He recognized a vaguely human shape to it: a head with chin tucked to chest, arms crossed over torso, legs tucked into stomach. But as Whistler studied the thing he realized that it couldn't be human.

The fingers and toes were too long compared to the palm and sole, the head was slightly too long and slightly too thin. Unraveled from its current position the thing would stand well over seven feet tall. The skin that was exposed (the hands, the feet, and, at this angle, the left ear) was papery, almost translucent. If the thing's veins had been red and blue they would have been clearly visible. As it was, Whistler thought the veins were gray.

The thing was wearing a hooded robe of pure white, but as Whistler's eyes recovered and the glowing continued to subside he realized that the white fabric was nuanced with a thousand colors, a prismatic garb the likes of which he had never dreamed before, let alone seen.

The fallen thing started to move and Whistler, frozen in place again, began shifting his eyes, looking carefully for his scythe. Any creature that could survive a fall like that had to be dangerous.

The thing unfolded slowly, its movements looking more plant than animal. It put its long hands to the ground and pushed itself onto hands and knees. Even in that position it was almost up to Whistler's waist, and he had never been called a short man.

The creature stood up with a soft grunt and wobbled on its feet for a moment. Then its eyes looked down and found Whistler, who still hadn't moved.

The creature's face was calm and smooth with a thin nose and white lips. Not sickly white like maggots, but pure white like fine paper. Two golden lines ran vertically from the thing's chin to its forehead, passing through its eyes, the irises of which were golden to match the lines.

"Where am I?" the thing asked as it brushed its long hands over its rumpled robe. Its voice was masculine and not unpleasant.

Whistler said nothing but looked around to see if there were others here. Not other creatures like this fallen thing, but other people. Someone to tell him he wasn't insane, to tell him they saw the same thing. There were no other people. He hadn't expected there to be.

"Salem, Nebraska," Whistler answered eventually as the thing waited expectantly.

"No," the creature said gently. "What planet?"

"Earth," Whistler said.

The creature looked around, its large, thin head moving strangely on its slightly-too-long neck.

"What year?" it asked. "That's the system you use here? Years?"

"Eighteen-eighty-four," Whistler said.

"So this is the Elemental Era," the thing said.

"I don't know what that is."

"No, no. Of course you haven't a frame of reference for that. But you may have to learn, Venturer. I have much to teach you in what could be a very short time."

"Gonna need to talk to me while I work. I got a cow that needs to be milked," Whistler said.

"Yes, yes I suppose that's alright," the creature said. He cocked his head to the side. "It's coming back to me. Memory is always so fuzzy after a fall like that. Earth. Yes. I remember now how I have always loved you humans. Your tenacity. Your understanding. Your adaptability. Well. Lead on. Introductions while we walk?" The creature didn't wait for a reply. "I'm an angel," it said. "Pick the holy book of your choice, remove the wings that everyone seems bent on giving us, and I am a Being straight from its pages."

The angel extended its hand and Whistler took it. The appendage looked so thin and frail in his, but he knew instinctively that no matter how hard he squeezed it he would never be able to break it. The long fingers folded almost all the way around his hand as he shook it up and down slowly.

"The human greeting of this era," the angel said. "I

like it. It is nice. Do you have a name?"

"Call me Whistler."

The angel raised a pale eyebrow. "So, Whistler," he said, withdrawing his hand, "now that you've summoned me-"

"Summoned you?" Whistler asked.

"Yes," the angel said. "The melody you whistled. You heard it from the Wind, I assume. It called me to you. It's not unusual for a human to develop powers that way, but they are rarely discovered, and even more rarely heard about, especially in the country of eighteen-eighties Nebraska. For you see, the Wind always pinpoints Venturers such as yourself."

Whistler held up his hands. He wasn't used to this much talking. He hadn't heard so many words in a row in over three years. "If you insist on gabbin' ya must know that I wasn't kiddin' about the cow." Whistler sighed. "You said we could walk. Follow me down to the barn if you must and you can finish talking to me there. Don't be mad if I don't get it right away, though."

"Oh," the angel said. "It's not really my way to get mad. Anger accomplishes nothing in the Realms that I come from."

Whistler shrugged. "I've seen it accomplish far too much on Earth."

With that he turned and started walking to the barn. *I'm never drinkin' again,* he thought.

△

Whistler *had* been kidding about the cow.

She didn't need to be milked again until after supper, but the angel didn't seem to know that and Whistler wasn't about to tell him. The simple, repetitive action of milking would help him think. He did some of his best thinking while milking, but the animal certainly never appreciated Whistler's thoughts. Maybe this angel would.

If he was real.

If anything was real.

Whistler had heard of people having episodes where they saw angels. He'd never believed them. Normally he chalked it up to instability, emotional distress, too much boozing. But now here he was, suffering their plight. *How much of a wreck am I?* His head felt a little fuzzy, but he wasn't still drunk. At least, he didn't think he was.

And besides, he'd been drunk plenty of times without meeting angels.

Whistler half-expected to turn around and see nothing, maybe be able to write this whole thing off as a strange hallucination, but he heard the slow footsteps behind him in the grass. The angel's long legs didn't have to take many strides to keep up.

Whistler reached the barn, a building of mottled red and white. The paint was peeling a bit, but overall it was a sound structure that could stand for fifty more years barring a tornado or fire. The thick beams had been felled and carved from trees that had been planted back when this area had still been part of the Nebraska Territory. Whistler remembered helping his father and the other men build it over forty years ago, climbing the skeleton of boards to the thrilling heights of it to attach more and more lumber. Every man had his fears, but heights had never been one of Whistler's.

Sunlight poured in through the door as Whistler pulled it open. He could see the dust motes in the air and they reminded him of the way the angel's robe shimmered.

The angel had to duck to get through the door, but only slightly, nodding his head down so the tip of his hood was the perfect distance from the top of the doorway as he passed under it.

Whistler went to the far wall, got the bucket that he used for grain and dunked it into the reserve he kept. He poured the grain loudly into a wooden trough and heard the clack and swish of it. His cow would hear too.

"Are cows still as shaggy and graceful as I remember them being?" the angel asked.

Whistler couldn't tell if it was a joke or not. This angel certainly seemed to have trouble remembering certain things. Whistler shook his head.

When the cow walked into the barn the angel seemed genuinely curious about her. "I must have my time periods confused," he muttered to himself. "Or my planets."

When the cow didn't react to the angel, Whistler got a sinking feeling in his stomach. That was strong evidence of hallucination. Cattle weren't the smartest animals, but they were uncannily in tune with their environment. No one but Whistler had been inside that barn for a long time, and the cow should have reacted to that.

"You're not real, are you?" Whistler asked as he sat on his sturdy three-legged stool and began to milk the brown jersey into a dented pail.

The angel stood silently.

"Well?" Whistler said.

"Oh," the angel said. "I'm sorry. I thought you were talking to the cow and I was most confused. No, I am real. A lot of Heroes probably think that angels are illusions at first. But I assure you that I am not."

Shing.

Shing.

Shing.

The milk rang in the pail.

The angel waited patiently.

"Alright," Whistler said. "Say what you've come to say to me and I'll do my best to cooperate. You . . . called me a hero? That made my ears prick up a bit."

The angel laughed gently. "Not a hero, Whistler. A Hero."

"Doesn't matter if you emphasize it."

"It does. You're on a different level from the other word. Do you understand?"

Shing.

"Nope."

Shing.

Shing.

"A hero is just a person," the angel said. "But a *Hero* has the ability - the fate - to change the world for the better."

"So I'm a Hero," Whistler said slowly. "Don't feel too heroic. Feel insane. Like I shoulda spent more time talkin' to that doctor that came through these parts all those years ago."

The angel laughed gently. "Oh, but you were born a Hero, Whistler. Let's just have that set and established. Only Heroes call angels, so you are a Hero. Accept it. Start thinking like it. You're the first of four."

"Four?"

"This part you will understand well," the angel said. "There are four elements. Earth, Water, Fire, and the one that helped you summon me, Wind."

Whistler understood. They were classifications that made sense. He had often thought about the interactions of the forces of the world. He'd had a lot of time to think in the past three years. It was amazing how much thinking you could get done when no one was around to derail your thoughts.

"Makes sense," Whistler said. "I'm with ya on that."

"Alright," the angel said. He hadn't moved at all, didn't seem restless standing in one spot, never shifted from one leg to the other, just stood. "The elements of your planet are governed by four powerful beings. I don't know their full workings since I'm not privy to that Realm, but I do know that they search for Heroes in their own way. It seems you have been found by Wind. It means you're what they call a Venturer, whether you know it or not. Wind knows who you are, has probably always known."

Whistler grunted and shifted his feet in the layer of straw that covered the barn floor. "Woulda thought myself Earth," he said.

"Now you're in the spirit of it!" the angel said excitedly. "You're wrong, though. You're not Earth. It's not what's on your outside, but what's on your inside that's important. Venturers long for adventure. No, it's not right to say they long for it, but rather that they adapt very quickly to it once it comes to them."

"I ain't goin' anywhere," Whistler said stubbornly, squeezing the cow hard enough to annoy her for a moment.

"You deny yourself," the angel said. "That's to be expected. But the sooner you can allow yourself to believe me, the easier everything will be." The angel stood silently for a moment and then asked, "Was this your father's farm?"

Whistler paused his milking for a moment. "Yes," he answered quietly.

"And, before he died, you promised him you'd keep the place for him, I assume. Or maybe it wasn't an overt promise, but just an understanding."

"I don't like people diggin' in my past," Whistler warned.

"You've been tied here," the angel said, moving slowly across the floor. "Maybe in more ways than you know. But your spirit longs to be *free*, Whistler. You're in

shackles here. You ever been south? North? East? West?
What's the farthest you've been from this place?
Something's kept you here. More than one thing.
Relationships. Failures. Stubbornness. What's holding you
back, Whistler? What's keeping you-"

Whistler shot up from his stool, tipping it over.
"Enough!" he bellowed. The cow swung her head around to
look at him.

"I am sorry," the angel said. "But you need to be
able to talk to me if I am to prepare you for the days ahead."

There was a pause in which both life forms looked at
each other; the angel from his golden eyes and Whistler
from his gray. A rooster crowed in the distance.

"Sorry," Whistler said. "But I did warn you. Give
me a minute, would ya?"

The angel waited while Whistler righted the stool
and sat back down on it. His mind was spinning, working
faster than it had in a decade, trying to decide what was true,
what was real, and what was craziness. But he was intrigued.
Something inside was already excited about the idea of
adventure.

"You can talk again," Whistler said.

"Good," the angel said. "You are a Venturer. Now
that I call attention to it . . . do you feel it?"

Whistler shrugged. "Maybe," he said. He sat
silently, milking. The angel waited. He seemed to be good
at that. Whistler spoke again. "In truth I've always wanted
to . . . see the world. But I was born here. I'll die here,
angel. You're right about one thing. I've made promises,
and I've work to do here. There are those that want this
land, angel. This land was my father's and I'll not see it ill-
used."

"Before your father, the land belonged to someone
else," the angel reminded him gently. "Or no one. You may

need to detach yourself from it soon, Whistler, if we are going to do what we need to do."

The cow was dry but still Whistler kept up the motion. "And what is it that we need to do?" he asked.

"That's not something that either of us knows yet," the angel said. "But it is a righteous task. There's always good work to be done for there are evils in this world beyond what you know."

"I know about evil, angel."

"I didn't say you didn't."

"I know about honor and loyalty and hard work and sacrifice and pain and everything they teach in that book of yours. I've got a Bible inside the house if you'd like to see it."

"Well," the angel said, "the things we're likely going to be faced with aren't in your Bible. Those chapters were burned a thousand years ago. Scoured clean. Sometimes it's safer not to know."

"How can it be safer to not know your enemy?" Whistler asked.

"Knowledge is dangerous. You would agree. Sometimes things are better left unknown, unbothered, unstirred. But look. I will reveal things only as I think you need to know them. This next: you're going to meet three other people – three other Heroes - and once you're all together you'll be able to do what it is that you need to do."

"I've no great pool of friends," Whistler noted, "and I have to warn you that not many people come 'round here. It might take years for me to meet the people you want me to meet. I'm not keen on folk."

"They might not come to you," the angel said. "You might go to them."

"I've no reason to leave here, angel. We've been over this. If I leave this place it dies. Do you understand?" He was getting dangerously agitated again, but a bit excited at the same time.

"They don't send angels to Earth for amusement, Whistler. It costs a great deal. I'm not to be taken lightly. If you're unwilling to bend, if you're unwilling to do what needs doing when the time comes, then I fear for the worst and-"

Something crashed through the wall of the barn with a great boom, sending chunks of wood flying through the air like the arrows of an angry god.

⌂ CHAPTER 2 ⌂

The ground rushed up and slammed into Whistler's back. He lay stunned until the pain set in and shocked him back to life. He pushed himself up and ripped out a long chunk of wood that had embedded itself in his forearm, and another from his thigh. That one had punctured clean through his work trousers.

"Damn," he cursed as he watched his blood flow. But there was no time to say more.

Something flew at him and he threw himself to the side without thinking. The wind was knocked out of him for a second time as he landed on the ground.

The cow was making an awful noise and Whistler saw that she was so riddled with splinters that she probably wouldn't survive. A large one had jammed itself deep into her eye socket, and the poor thing was rubbing her head against the ground trying to get it out.

Think, Whistler, think. Survive.

Whistler scrambled backwards, determined to defend himself against whatever was happening. He reached behind him and his hand fell on a pitchfork. He rose with difficulty and scanned the barn for any sign of the attacker, brandishing the pitchfork in two hands.

There was nothing. No attacker, no angel.

But Whistler heard the sounds of fighting just outside.

"Sorry, girl," Whistler said to the cow. "I'll get whoever did this to ya."

He rushed out into the light.

⌂

The angel was flowing and twirling, his long limbs moving fluidly through the air. His fingers were tipped with claws that hadn't been there before and his body had swelled up. Where it had been delicate, it was now bulky.

When Whistler looked to see what the angel was fighting, his blood froze. He didn't need the angel to tell him what it was.

First an angel . . . now a demon.

The first thing that struck Whistler about the demon was its mouth, which was far too large and eerily human. The jaw looked as if would be able to unhinge like a snake's, making Whistler feel that the demon had the capability to swallow him whole if it had wanted to. And it looked like it wanted to. Its teeth were sharp, broken into shattered points. Whistler was unsure if the demon's mouth could actually close properly or if it was permanently stuck in a drooling rictus.

The body wasn't right, like the angel's wasn't right, but in the opposite way. Where the angel was graceful, the demon was grotesque. Broken bones stuck out through its black and red skin, but Whistler couldn't tell if it bothered the demon at all. The injuries would have probably killed a man, but it seemed to be the demon's natural state.

Whistler stood dumbly with his pitchfork while the angel and demon danced.

"It's too soon!" the angel shouted. "You've got to run and get away from here, Whistler! As far as you can get!"

The angel's claws raked the demon's shoulder and it howled, then the angel lurched backwards, avoiding the counterstrike by a hair.

Whistler knew that he would be stupid to blindly rush that enemy. He could barely follow the swift movements of the angel, let alone the demon. Putting himself into the middle of that would be suicide.

He started to run for the horses, his arm and leg pouring blood onto the green grass.

This was real. This was all much, much too real.

How much could I be imagining? he thought, wishing he could find some way to wake up. *Have I gone insane like Raving Bill? The man chewed through his own cheeks in his madness before they could subdue him.*

The pain in Whistler's leg was too great. He tried to grit his teeth through it but he couldn't and had to stop running before he passed out. Pausing, panting, he threw his pitchfork down. The weapon wouldn't be of any use. He looked behind him.

The demon was climbing the side of the barn now, clawing its way up as boards came loose and fell to the earth. The angel followed with his long, powerful arms.

The horses were still far off. Whistler took his handkerchief out of his pocket and tried to tie it around his leg wound, hoping he might be able to walk if he could just bind it together. He'd never been terribly adept at mending. His strategy had always been to let things fix themselves, but there was no time for that now. He had to pull himself together while he still could.

Whistler's fingers fumbled. The wound in his forearm screamed. He couldn't get the handkerchief to tie tightly enough, and the pain was incredible. He screamed a curse and dropped the cloth on the ground.

He heard the demon howling and glanced back again. The monster had reached the apex of the barn. It stood like a proud cock and roared, its already large mouth open almost to its waist, a nerve-grating sound issuing from its throat. As the monster howled, the sky darkened above it. The clear day was suddenly overcast with an expanding, swirling roil of black clouds.

A wave of death rolled out from the barn. The building's strong boards withered and rippled, popped and hissed. Nails flew through the air like bullets. The grass began to die. Anything that was alive - or had once been alive - was rotting in response to the demon. The wave of destruction rippled outward, annihilating everything it touched.

The angel moved across the top of the barn, bracing himself against the demonic death wave that threatened to rend the world. He alone was pure and untouched by the demon's onslaught.

My life is over, Whistler thought. U*nless I get away.*

Lightning struck and thunder cracked. He felt it try to deafen him. Over and over, flash and boom, faster and more fearsome than almost any storm he had yet lived through.

He tried to take a step but his leg buckled and he fell onto his knee.

And now the horses were running the opposite way. *I have to get one of 'em.* But there was no way the horses would hear him over the chaos, let alone come *towards* the destruction.

But I ain't dyin' now.

The wave of death was nearing him. Whistler put his fingers in his mouth and - praying that the horses would obey - blew a mighty note to call them.

Wheeooo-wheeeeeet!

The sound echoed through the open world somehow, piercing the storm with a power that it should not have had. Whistler watched the horses react to it. They turned and ran back towards him, ramming at the fence with their chests. Normally the barrier would have been enough to keep them in, even in its worn state, but now they were determined to get out.

It's my power, Whistler thought, looking down at his fingers. *The angel was right. The power of wind. Of breath.*

Whistler readied himself to jump. No horse was saddled right now and he would have to do this one-armed and one-legged.

The horses broke free and ran towards him with terrified eyes, Whistler's magic propelling them in a direction that they clearly did not wish to go. He Whistled again to urge them on. Black was in the lead as Whistler had known he would be. The stallion was no draft horse like the other two were. Black was for riding. He was for speed.

Whistler launched himself off the ground with one leg as Black neared him. The horse turned sideways and Whistler grabbed his mane with his left hand in one smooth motion. His left leg screamed with pain as he hauled himself onto the stallion's back.

Black's hooves were inches away from the expanding destruction as he wheeled and - in a single great burst of speed - shot off to the southwest.

Whistler looked back to see the other two horses get swallowed by the expanding ripple of death. They screamed as their skin was stripped off by invisible hands, blood flying through the air, bones falling to the ground.

"Run!" Whistler yelled to Black over the booming thunder. "RUN!"

Then he buried his face in Black's mane and prayed.

Whistler rode Black until the horse nearly collapsed. It wasn't Whistler's fault. He had tried several times to stop the horse, but the poor thing was terrified, shaking and shuddering even as it galloped.

Finally the horse slowed and Whistler clicked for him to stop. Then the farmer carefully and painfully rolled from Black's back onto the soft prairie grasses and lay panting. He looked back to the northeast, fearful that he would see the black demonic clouds swelling towards him. He didn't. Maybe the hallucination was over, or maybe he had passed deeper into madness.

Whistler's pants were stuck to his leg with blood, but at least the gash had stopped gushing. It was numb now, which he supposed was probably a good thing. He crawled gingerly towards where Black was gulping water from a nearby stream. The horse's ears were still flattened back against his head, and he still looked as if he wanted to bolt, but it was drink or die and the horse knew it.

Whistler managed to get a palm-full of water to his own mouth.

Is this the same stream that runs west of my place? he wondered.

It could have been. The water tasted the same. But Whistler didn't *really* know where he was. He hadn't been paying attention during Black's mad dash.

This could be Kansas by now. He checked the position of the sun, trying to determine what time of day it was, doing the math on how far Black might have run. Had he gone straight southwest the whole way? It might have been so.

There was no one around. He'd seen nothing during his flight. He hadn't been this direction in thirty years and it was still the same: no people, no buildings, no sign of nature tamed.

He had thought that by rarely leaving his home - by being almost completely self-reliant - he was avoiding the humanity which he had grown so jealous of. He had become envious of the way it thrived, the way it didn't give up. The way it seemed to carry on easily while he had always struggled.

He had expected settlements all around him. He'd always been worried to wake up one day to see neighbors coming onto his property to introduce themselves. These imaginary people would have had children, ten of them. The brats would be climbing all over the place. Whistler would have kicked them out of his fields.

None of that had ever happened, though, and by the look of this calm, quiet country, it hadn't even come close to happening.

He could have given himself a much wider berth.

Have I truly been that blind? What happened *to me after she left?*

Whistler had to admit to himself that despite the terror of all that had just transpired he felt rather excited. The freedom, if one could call it that, was intoxicating.

What did the angel call me? A Venturer? Maybe I am *that, after all.*

He felt all manner of confusion, mixed emotions.

Whistler lay on his side, exhausted from the simple act of drinking water, and fell asleep.

△

Whistler's dreams were filled with images so terrifying that he awoke again almost immediately.

He was sweating now, and his arm was stuck to the grass with blood. He pried it loose and clumsily picked the grass from it with stubby fingers.

Black had found a shady tree not far off and was laying there, fully passed out on his side, legs splayed out.

Whistler watched the horse's chest rise and fall a few times to make sure he still lived, and then tried to right himself.

Dizziness greeted him with a nauseating handshake as he struggled to be vertical. He looked to the northeast again. He didn't see anything out of the ordinary.

Thoughts of the angel came to him then, and he felt a pang of responsibility. Now that he had seen to himself he had room to worry about another. Surely an angel could handle things, but the white creature had certainly looked outmatched . . .

The wind blew through Whistler's hair, reminding him.

Whistler brought his dry lips together and blew the melody he'd heard earlier that day. Then he stopped, remembering how the angel had arrived, and got slowly to his feet so that he could move if he had to. He couldn't bend his left knee, but he could stand and shuffle a bit.

Once prepared, he continued to whistle the melody over and over again as he had before. This time, though, he had control, knew what he was doing, what might happen when he finished. He concentrated on a spot near the stream's edge, imagining how the angel might look there.

One time. Two times. Three.

A streak of light flew towards the spot, not from the air this time, but across the ground. The grasses parted with the wind of its passing. It also wasn't as bright this time, but it *was* the angel.

He was a disaster.

He knelt on the ground, black and white liquids dripping from his face. His robe was shredded and covered in filth. He was holding a twisted piece of wood in his hand. "Thank God," he whispered, as the light faded from him.

The angel looked the way that Whistler felt: haggard

and beaten.

"Did ya kill it?" Whistler asked, not really knowing what to say.

The angel nodded and winced. He managed, with a pained look, to situate himself on the ground. He sat cross-legged, the posture looking child-like even when worn by one so large as the angel. He breathed slowly in and out.

"How?" Whistler asked.

The angel reached into his robe and pulled out a small black-green wad of flesh. It looked like a shriveled, shrunken heart.

"You either crush the heart or remove it. I chose both." The angel put the organ back into his robe. "After I killed it," he said weakly, "I climbed down from your barn. I went to look for you, but you weren't there. My legs weren't working particularly well and I didn't know which direction you had gone. My only hope was that you would summon me again. I was able to quickly search your field for useful objects and even made it into your house briefly. Your property . . . your home . . . is a festering spot of land now. But I managed to get your sword."

The angel raised the twisted piece of wood he was holding, and it was only then that Whistler realized it was his scythe. The silver blade and wooden handle had both been blackened by the demon's wave of death, and both were twisted, as if wrung by giant hands.

"It's . . . not a very good weapon, angel," Whistler said cautiously. "You said you went into my house. You didn't find my gun?"

The angel placed the scythe on the ground and then put his bleeding face into his hands. "No, I didn't. I don't know how this works," he moaned. "When I talked about the Heroes. The elements. This quest of ours. That was true. But my truth ends there. I thought I would have time . . . to figure this out. But the last truth I have left is . . . that I've never done this before."

"Done what before?" Whistler asked.

"This." The angel gestured with arms wide open. "I've never been to Earth before. I know the terminology, the basic concepts, but I get confused sometimes. My knowledge is like a muscle. The more I flex it the stronger it gets. Apparently I knew enough to be sent. To be summoned. But beyond that . . ." He made an empty gesture to the northeast. "I don't even know what I fought back there."

"Demon," Whistler grunted.

"Oh, but there are so many kinds," the angel said woefully. "The way it fought leads me to believe it was a Desolator. But . . . if I recall correctly that's a fairly high-ranking creature to be sending after a Hero. Unless you're a Worldbreaker, Whistler, and I don't think you are." The angel squinted at him. "No, they wouldn't send a new angel like me to look after a Worldbreaker. Wouldn't be right."

"But you do know things," Whistler pointed out. "Who taught you what you know?"

"We aren't taught. Not in an academy, or . . . I suppose you would call them schoolhouses, Whistler. We angels are born with a near limitless framework for intelligence, but very little actual knowledge. We know terms, jargon, concepts. The way we apply our knowledge grows with time and Mission. And I haven't had time. I'm new. I'm too new." The angel hung his head. He was still leaking white-gold blood. "There are many metaphors I could use. It's like waking up. It's like stretching. It's like a recurring dream that haunts me. It's *like* I've done this before. But I never have.

"So there's my confession." The angel sighed. "I'm actually glad it worked out this way. Now I can just admit I don't know what I'm doing."

"You cost me my farm," Whistler said. He should have been angry, but he found that being untethered was rather invigorating. His excitement met his pain and they canceled each other out.

"It may be," the angel said. "And for that I am eternally sorry. But what's equally likely is that I showed up just in time to salvage what I could from a place destined for Desolation." He reached into his robe and pulled something from it. It was a picture frame that Whistler hadn't seen in years. He'd put it away in a drawer, left it to rot. The angel pointed to the picture that it contained. "I'm getting a strong Feeling from this," he said. "I've told you my secrets, Whistler. Now . . . you have to tell me yours." He paused, gently tapping the glass. "Who is she?"

"I already warned you about this," Whistler said.

"The time for warnings is over, Whistler. Our . . . honeymoon is over. Tell me who she is, and quickly."

Whistler found that his hands were shaking even more than they had been during the demon's attack. He didn't like this, not one bit. But he couldn't go back to his home. The place he'd lived for his entire life was likely blackened and rotten. His animals dead, his crops withered, his house (although it had never been much) was likely a husk.

What do I have left to lose?

He felt his throat starting to tighten and he looked away from where the angel sat. He looked at Black, and the steady breathing of the large animal reassured him. He turned back to the angel.

"Alright," Whistler said. "I'll tell ya. But it ain't gonna be quick. And it ain't gonna be easy."

△

"She was everything," Whistler began. He picked a piece of nearby grass and stuck the end in his mouth. "You know what love is, angel?"

The angel nodded.

"No ya don't," Whistler said. "You don't know the half of it. But *I* know. We were married at fifteen. That's a long time to spend with someone, ya know? I mean really *with* someone. All the time. Everyday. Homesteadin' demands time and effort; two people workin' together, feedin' off each other's talents and energy.

"It was excitin'. We were just two creatures tryin' to make it work, like we'd seen our own parents do. Knew it could be done. Knew it was possible. Thought I knew what I needed to know. But the stuff my daddy had to deal with never seemed to happen to me. The stuff I was equipped to handle never came. So I was left forging my own path when I thought it had been trampled for me already. Well, there was always somethin' goin' wrong and it was her – the woman in that photo - that kept liftin' me up.

"This one time my cattle were gettin' sick, angel. Real sick. The whole lot of 'em. We had more back then; a herd of six. Couldn't afford to lose any. My daddy'd been long dead by then so I couldn't go to him for advice, ya know, and eventually the disease claimed a cow. Was the woman in that picture who found the tiny cuts on her legs. A few rusty nails stickin' out of a post were cuttin' 'em as they walked by, sticking their heads over the fence so they could graze just outside of their boundaries. That's what was causin' the disease.

"I swear to ya more crops failed than succeeded. Always some damn critters gettin' into 'em and it was all I could do to make ends meet.

"Had a few terrible tornadoes. The kind that leave

dug-out trails in the earth. Sometimes the ground afterwards looked like a hundred men with shovels had been out there diggin' with a frenzy. Trees tipped over, everything flattened. Lost a good chunk of my house one year. But I built it again because that's what you do.

"Fires can come streaking across the prairie with a speed you wouldn't believe, angel. The animals warn ya. They run ahead of the blaze, whole packs of 'em. If you see a thousand jackrabbits comin' at ya, you *dig*, angel. You get a shovel and you dig. Dig a ditch so the fire can't get through and eat your life."

"Tornadoes and flame. The Wind and The Fire," the angel noted.

"Hey," Whistler said. "Don't interrupt now."

"I apologize."

"Well, the point is, she kept me going through it all," Whistler said, gesturing at the picture in the frame that the angel still held. "Somehow, every year we made it, just barely. Maybe that's the way life's supposed to be. Just makin' it. Barely. Or maybe we were just happy failures." Whistler breathed out. "Because we *were* happy. You know what happiness is?"

"No," the angel said with a hint of a smile.

"Now yer gettin' the hang of this," Whistler said. "I remember there was one summer we almost died," he chuckled, the memories flooding back. "Bear came into my house one night. Strangest thing. Don't get bears in these parts. Thought it was gonna kill us, but it didn't. It looked us over. It mighta been sick, I don't know. It left after the most terrifying staring contest of my life. My heart was beatin' so fast I thought it would explode and kill me where the bear hadn't.

"But I made it. I didn't die that day.

"There was one winter where the snow didn't melt.

Didn't melt for so long that I feared the world would stay frozen forever. Course I never woulda told *her* I felt that way. Never much room for thinkin' like that when you got survivin' to do. I was considerin' eatin' sawdust near the end of that winter. But we made it, ya know? As far as we were concerned, everything was goin' our way. I haven't had that feeling in so long . . . but I remember what it felt like." Whistler put a hand to his chest. His emotions were making it hurt. He chuckled nervously. "It's been long buried. Like a coffin that don't wanna be opened."

"So what happened with her?" the angel asked.

"I'm gettin' there," Whistler said. "But I don't wanna be gettin' there."

The angel waited.

Whistler spat out his grass and watched the long reed fall to the ground. "Do you create life? Up in heaven, I mean?"

"Well, it's complicated," the angel responded.

"Yeah. That's what I found out, too. Well . . . alright. We were comin' to find that a farm needed warm hearts and strong hands. The more the merrier. I myself had five siblings, she had three. Was the thing to do. Family and all that. We'd been at it alone long enough.

"So . . . we tried to create life. Here on Earth. The method is well known among all living things. Well, she was pregnant, you know. And then not too far into it, it was over. Baby didn't make it, angel. You ever . . . you ever see it up there?" Whistler looked at the sky.

"It doesn't work that way," the angel said.

"No," Whistler said, his voice thin. "I guess not. Well. We tried again. Didn't work. Tried again. Didn't work. Every season was torture. We blamed ourselves. Each other. Other folk. The weather. The water. Finally somethin' sparked again, burned hot like an ember on long-dead coals, and then it was . . . over again."

Whistler felt his eyes getting wet and warm. He stared straight ahead. He had come too far to stop the telling now.

"After that it was more blame, more pain. Always that layer of pain that ate at us like locusts on a good crop. Took us nearly four years and many, many yelling arguments, to finally get and lose the fifth pregnancy."

Whistler paused, and breathed out slowly.

"We must have been lunatics to try a sixth time," he said. "As mad as a couple o' Raving Bills. Got too far that final time. She was big in the stomach, ya know. Toddling about. Leaning back to stretch. She was hot or cold or mad or happy all in a manner of minutes." Whistler laughed mirthlessly, his throat tightening. "It looked like maybe . . ."

He clenched his fists.

"But that one didn't work either. This time, though, there was a baby. A girl. I saw the dead thing. God help me, I saw it. I held it. I had to bury it. I dug it a hole and I *put it in*." Whistler's tears were streaming down his face. "Well . . . that was the last time we tried.

"That killed us. That was it. The winter we could do. The winds. The fires. The plagues. Droughts. Any danger. Any hunger. But that baby, almost fully formed . . . that we couldn't do. Twenty years later the woman in that picture left. Don't know where she went. I remember I was sittin' on the porch scraping chicken crap off the bottom of my shoes with a stick when she rode off. No words. Nothin'. But I knew. She knew. We knew.

"And I know what *yer* thinkin', angel. Twenty years is a long time. Couldn't it have been somethin' else? Some other reason she left? But the weight of it pressed on us over those years and drove a wedge between us that not even

Bunyan himself coulda yanked out. Sometimes it's the things you *don't* talk about that destroy you, angel. Near the end we couldn't even look each other in the eyes. Never forgave ourselves. For trying so hard? For being so stubborn or . . . or so hopeful? I don't know.

"It was just three years ago when she left, but when I think about it now, well, it's like lookin' back on someone else's life. I'm two different people. The man before. And the man after.

"And that's who she was."

Whistler stared at the ground, his vision blurred by tears. He'd never told anyone the things he had just said. His own family was scattered, two of his brothers dead in the Rockies, the others with fates unknown to him. There had been no one to share his pain with.

"The woman in the picture," the angel said after a little while. "Did she have a name?"

"Yeah," Whistler said. "Yeah, she did."

And that was the last he would say on the subject.

△ CHAPTER 3 △

It was several hours later and Whistler had just awakened in another cold sweat after an agonizingly short bit of sleep. Now he was washing his wounds in the cold stream water as the beautiful sun began to set. The angel still looked in bad shape. His walking and movements weren't nearly as fluid as they had been when he'd first arrived on Earth. Whistler thought that the Desolator had taken a greater toll on the angel than he was letting on.

"There must be a clue somewhere," the angel said.

"A clue?" Whistler asked.

"Yes. We . . . well, we need to find out where we should be going, what we should be doing. And soon, I think. The longer we stay still the longer the demons have to find us and kill us. That's their job, you know."

"I didn't assume anything but," Whistler said. He limped away from the stream and picked up his twisted, blackened scythe. It was little more than an unwieldy club. A scythe's cutting edge faces the man who holds it. It wouldn't be a very good weapon, but it was all Whistler had. Black was standing up now, eating grass, eyes looking around warily. He seemed to slowly be regaining trust in his surroundings. "I can move again if you can. I'd rather be in discomfort than meet another demon."

"And I as well. But I haven't any idea where to go," the angel said. "I didn't have enough of a chance to rummage through your house before you Called me here. There might have been clues in there that would've set us on our path. More items I might have had Feelings about. There's a chance we could go back there, but that . . . doesn't Feel right to me. The Desolation might take a while to wear off of that area. It might be best . . . not to go anywhere near it." The angel was deep in thought, his face scarred and strange. He'd washed the white blood and the other, much darker demon blood away, but he was a far cry from pristine. He stood still while Whistler began to bandage his own wounds. Then, out of a dead stillness, the angel snapped his long fingers in an uncharacteristically human manner. "You're a Venturer," he said.

"We've established that," Whistler replied.

"You follow the wind, Whistler. Tell me. What's the largest tornado you've ever known?"

Whistler didn't even need to think about it. "Five years ago," he said. "Came in from the southwest. Winds fit to tear the sod from the earth. Tossed cattle like they were toys, wood fences like they were paper. Everything in its path: destroyed. Rumor was that it picked up a barn and threw it down in one piece an entire county away. Blew itself out just northeast of my property. Never seen anything like it."

"A . . . tee-five," the angel muttered.

"What's that?"

"Nothing. Nothing. Something from a different time. It came from the southwest, you say?" The angel gazed off in that direction. "That's the direction that you fled. I doubt it's a coincidence. Did you ever hear where that tornado originated?"

"Long about down in Kansas somewhere," Whistler said. "I heard it made a path a hundred miles long."

"And how well do you think you could follow that path?"

Whistler shrugged. "If I had ta guess I'd say not well at all. But I know which way is southwest if that's any help." Whistler had finished wrapping his own wounds so he checked Black over. The horse was tired and still skittish, but he wasn't injured. "We're gonna have to trap something," Whistler said, stomach rumbling. Most of his food had come from his own garden and his animals, but he had learned survival from his father and figured he could hold his own out here in the wilderness, even without a gun. "Do you need to eat?"

The angel shook his head. "No, but you should, Whistler. You'll need all the strength you can get."

"I'll get on it if you'll do me one favor."

"What's that?" the angel asked.

"Throw that picture in the stream. I don't want it with us."

The angel frowned thoughtfully for a moment and then complied. The frame hit the water with a tiny slap.

Whistler watched the embodiment of his pain wash out of sight.

⚐ CHAPTER 4 ⚐

Whistler hadn't had the tools to skin and clean the rabbit properly, but he had been able to start a small fire and improvise. All in all it was a good meal. He wondered how long he would have to survive this way. This part of America might be sparsely populated, but eventually they'd have to come across a town, although Whistler didn't know what good that would do them. They couldn't resupply unless the angel had happened to grab any money from Whistler's house. He doubted that was the case.

Whistler wondered for the first time how other people would react to the angel. The angel didn't seem too concerned when Whistler asked.

"They'll either accept me or not see me at all," he said. "Their minds will write me off as a phantasm if they don't believe."

"So the fact that I can see you . . ."

"Means you are . . . *alright* with believing in me. If seeing me would damage someone's mind, they simply won't see me. Your cow was not alright with me. It did not see me."

"Sure," Whistler said. He looked at the setting sun. Night would be on them soon. "Should we start moving now? I know people usually sleep at night, but I don't want to hold still in the darkness if you know what I mean."

The angel stood slowly. "I think I can go on. Southwest. Feel your way along the path that the wind left for you so long ago, and watch for others. There will be three more that you'll need."

"That much you know."

"That much I know. I'm remembering more things. More Feelings. We follow the path of that wind."

Whistler patted Black's head and was able to mount after some difficulty. He had considered letting the horse go free, but a voice in his head reminded him to use every tool he had available to him. He had to be resourceful.

Whistler carried his scythe awkwardly in one hand. Besides his clothing, it was all he had. His mind – strengthened by endless routine – told him it was time to lock up the animals that needed locking up. But they were all dead. It was a painful thought. Maybe he'd have to get used to that, and quickly.

Whistler took a moment to orient himself and then set Black walking southwest.

Follow the wind, he thought. He listened for another melody, something powerful, but there was nothing. *It's as good an idea as any right now.*

Bareback riding drained him. Without a proper saddle to hang onto his arms and legs got tired, and the progress that he was making was slow. The angel walked along beside him, his long legs able to keep up easily. There did seem to be hitch in his gate and Whistler wondered just how injured the creature was.

Despite Whistler's zeal to escape he knew that if he kept pushing himself this hard he would end up like the angel, or worse. The angel wore a weary look and when Whistler asked if he wanted to stop and rest, the angel complied.

They found a tiny grove of shrubs to nestle into and were asleep by the time the moon was up.

⛢ CHAPTER 5 ⛢

"Wake up!" the angel shouted.

Whistler startled awake and tried to bolt upright, got tangled in some nettles and fell down again.

The demonic noises were back.

Damn! No!

Whistler struggled to his feet. The sun was just coming over the horizon and the whole prairie had long shadows on it. The grass was cold and wet, slippery. His own clothing was damp and uncomfortable. He grabbed his scythe with sleepy hands that had done far too much in the past half-day and he thought, *I'd rather die than live like this.* But only briefly, for then he saw the demon and his mind was shocked into action.

It was different than the first one. *Maybe not a Desolator this time.* It was a sickly pale color and resembled a large praying mantis. It had a shiny, hard carapace that was covered in nasty looking hooked thorns. Its limbs were thin, but Whistler didn't for a moment believe that it was weak.

The angel was already trying to attack it, but the demon was only toying with the exhausted figure in white. The angel struck out with long arms that were clearly tired and still damaged from his other fight.

Wheeoo-wheet!

Whistler waited and gripped his scythe tightly.

He whistled again. *Wheeoo-wheeeeet!*

Black came racing back from wherever he had run off to. Whistler felt bad for Black, but his own legs were shaky; he needed different ones. He hauled himself up and gave Black a gentle command. The horse charged the demon just as the vile creature landed a blow that sent the angel reeling backwards with a sickening crunch and a strangled scream.

"Back ta hell with ya!" Whistler bellowed as Black whirled around the demon.

Whistler swung his scythe out in a great arc, hoping to catch the demon in the head or neck. Anywhere, really, where he could do damage. It was a clumsy swing. The demon leaped back, quick as lightning, and then surged in again. Black danced out of the way. The horse was only under control because of the powerful whistled command that he had been given, else he would have bolted again. Whistler wouldn't have blamed him.

The angel was struggling to right himself. The demon screeched, his long serrated arms stabbing in and out, trying to catch Black's dancing legs.

If I don't get off, Black's gonna get shredded. If I get off I'm gonna get shredded.

Black was dodging wildly, terror in his eyes. The frenzied jostling was more than Whistler's wounded arm could take and he lost his grip. He turned his fall into a dive as best he could and landed in an awkward roll. "Dammit all," he cursed as he righted himself.

The demon was there in the blink of an eye and Whistler found himself with no options. He thought about trying to whistle, but didn't know what that would accomplish. He didn't hear any melodies on the air. There was no wind at all.

The demon dove on top of him, its mouth rife with six-inch, jagged teeth. Whistler kept the thing off of him with his scythe held sideways between his two hands. The blackened, twisted wood scraped against the cold, pale carapace of the demon with a nerve-grating noise.

The demon seemed to smile as it slowly worked its mouth towards Whistler's skull. He could see the back of its throat now, lined with barbs that pointed down into the darkness.

Whistler's arms started to give, his forearm wound screamed with new pain. It had broken open again and blood fell onto his face.

He wasn't sure he wanted to live a life harried by demons and considered just giving up, but decided against it. He'd been fighting demons his whole life, just not quite so literally. He pushed his scythe up with renewed vigor, feeling the tendons in his neck pop. Spots swam in front of his eyes as he strained. Suddenly the demon was flying, something heavy connecting with its carapace, cracking pieces off of it as it was hurled a good twenty feet away.

A strong hand grabbed Whistler's wrist and hauled him to his feet with ease.

The angel.

It wasn't the angel.

It was a massive, black-skinned man with deep layers of muscle. In one hand the man held Whistler's wrist, and in the other he held two huge hammers that looked quite suitable for driving railroad spikes.

"Stay back," the man said in a deep voice.

The demon was righting itself, struggling with its left shoulder, which had been shattered by the man's hammers.

The big man shifted one hammer into each hand, raised them high in the air and knocked the heads together. CLANG. CLANG CLANG.

Then he brought the hammers crashing to the ground.

BOOM!

The ground shook and rippled. A knee-high tidal wave of dirt and rocks careened towards the demon.

The man held his hammers high again and clicked the heads and shafts together in a rhythmic pattern.

CLANG! CLACKA CLANG-A-CLANG!

Then the man pounded the earth again.

BOOM!

Another wave issued forward. The man rode this second wave towards his enemy, his large feet spread out to help him balance on the rolling ground.

He reached the demon just as the monster lost its footing from the first earthen wave. The black man brought his hammers out to the side and then crashed the gleaming silver heads together swiftly. The blows struck the demon in both sides of its chest, crushing it with the sound of splintering wood.

The monster backpedaled and fell down gasping, trying to claw its way forward across the ground, its fingers digging into the soil, dark green blood leaking from ten different places.

The black man turned around before the monster was fully dead and shouldered his hammers; the silvery heads were covered in dark blood.

"Thank you," Whistler gasped.

"No problem, sir," the man said, walking over. He was smiling. "It's what I do. Got a bone ta pick with all demons: flesh or otherwise." He put both hammers in one hand and extended his other. Whistler took it. "I'd sure like ta know what yer doin' out in the middle o' nowhere runnin' from demons, but introductions always come first."

"Call me Whistler," Whistler said, awestruck at the strength of the man's grip.

"Howdy, Whistler," said the black man. "Name's John Henry. Now, what else can I do for ya?"

▽ PART 2: EARTH ▽

▽ CHAPTER 6 ▽

"How'd ya do that?" Whistler asked in amazement. He looked at the corpse of the repulsive demon.

"Took a lotta practice," John said. He gazed around. His eyes widened and his grip tightened on his hammers. "What's that?" He motioned towards where the angel sat against a tree.

The angel said people that believed would see and accept him.

"He's an angel," Whistler explained. "He means you no harm, and he's pretty beat up as it is."

"An angel, huh? It's about time!" John laughed. "Could use a little help 'round this place."

"Yeah," Whistler said. "See, I called him accidentally and now I'm on the run for my life. From demons."

"Yeah, I gathered," John said, his face grave for a moment. "I don't mind bustin' up demons. Been doin' it awhile now. You and I got somethin' in common."

"You're Earth," Whistler said. A chill ran up his spine. What the angel had said was coming true.

"Listen," John said, "I'm sure we got plenty to talk 'bout. But first we need to see to yer friend." He started walking slowly over to where the angel sat.

Now that the panic was over Whistler took a long look at John. The man was wearing heavy boots and overalls, both of which were dirty and faded. Under his overalls he wore a white shirt that may have at one time had gray stripes on it. A few ragged patches completed the ensemble.

He must be some sort of freed slave, Whistler thought. *It's more often a black man is free than slave now.* John had muscle upon muscle. His shoulders threatened to burst the straps of his overalls. His forearms were defined by strips of muscle that ran from elbow to wrist. Whistler felt instant respect.

John had reached the angel and Whistler caught up. The big man was trying to help the angel to his feet but he was struggling with the task and ultimately failed. John was strong, but the angel was a very large creature and not able to support himself much at all right now.

"You're . . . Earth," the angel said to John as the big black man was forced to set him down.

"One of you's gonna have to tell me what you mean," John said looking back and forth between the angel and Whistler.

The angel, looking even paler than usual, gestured to Whistler. So the farmer did the best he could to explain what had happened so far. He talked about his farm, the angel, his being a Venturer, his powers, and his brief journey down the supposed path of the tornado.

"Why can you do what you do?" he asked John when he had reached the end of his own story.

"You mean with my hammers?" John asked.

Whistler nodded.

"Don't know *why*, exactly," John admitted. "Never met anyone else that can do what I do. I was urged into developing the Touch by a friend of mine. Just felt it one day. Accidental. Once I accepted it I found I could make the earth move."

"You're a Forger, just as Whistler is a Venturer," the angel said. "You want to mend, John. Make things right. Just as Whistler wants to move, to see the world. We need to know about you. To hear your story."

"Shouldn't we move from this place?" Whistler asked.

"He do wanna go, don't he?" John asked the angel.

"Now that he has his freedom he can't resist the urge to travel," the angel replied.

"I just mean because the demons could be comin' for us," Whistler said. But he wasn't sure that he didn't just want to *move*.

"Never know when they gonna strike," John agreed. "One time I went a year without seein' one. Now I've killed three in as many days. But yer friend here can't move right now, Whistler. I can't carry him and you got wounds. Your horse don't look in much better shape. We need to rest."

"I assure you I can heal quickly," the angel said to Whistler. "Where your leg and arm wounds will last weeks, even months, my injuries can knit in mere hours if I rest. Give me a moment to breathe and we will be on our way again. In the meantime John, tell us who you are, what you know, and where you're going. Stories are important and Whistler's already told me his. Let's see what you have to say."

The black man nodded, set his hammers down, and then sat on the ground next to them.

And there he began his story, not more than fifty feet from the corpse of a demon.

"It started when I was a slave in the summer of fifty-two . . ."

▽ CHAPTER 7 ▽

John was sweating in the tiny shack that was his house. He shared it with nine others. The place would have been small for two people, let alone ten, and he knew too well that the North Carolina summers could sweat a man to death even in the open.

Even though John was only six years old he knew a few important things. He already knew how to work hard for his master. That was important, because if you didn't work hard you got the whip. He knew he had no mother and no father. A woman had made sure he'd survived infancy, but she had disappeared just as John had grown old enough to remember her face. It had been a face much like any other here: worn, tired, but somehow hopeful. Eventually she had died. Or escaped. Or been traded. It was hard to tell what happened to anyone around here. One day they simply *weren't*.

The sun was peeking over the horizon which meant that it was time to be about work in the tobacco fields. John grabbed a sack from the wall and was the first one out the door of the small shack.

His hands were sore. The tobacco demanded all of his time. It was year-round planting, nurturing, picking, and processing. There was tobacco as far as the eye could see. John had only seen the edge of the fields once. It had been like seeing the end of the world.

He walked out into the fields and started working. It didn't take any words to get him going. He knew what he had to do. He clicked his tongue as he worked. The rhythm of it helped to keep him distracted. The sun began to burn and the air was so humid that he may as well have been working underwater. In a few minutes his clothes were covered in a mixture of dust, sweat, and leaves. The world threatened to burn him up, but nothing could stop him once his tongue had the rhythm.

Click. Pick. Click. Pick. Click. Pick.

Now his feet joined in. Every step he took was a new part of his song. *Click. Step. Click Step Pick. Click. Step. Click Step Pick.*

He heard the swish of his arms against his thin shirt. *Swish Click Step Pick. Swish-a-swish-a Click Step. Step Pick.*

Other slaves would yell to each other in the fields, talking and carrying on, but John preferred to work alone, his rhythmic song his only company. He rarely spoke out loud. He used just enough words to get by.

Topping tobacco wasn't one of John's favorite jobs, but it wasn't awful. The stalks were about four feet tall, just a little over his head, and he could reach to pick the little cluster of leaves off the top. He didn't know why he was supposed to do it. No one had ever explained the purpose to him. But it was one of the things he could do well. He would later find out that there had been a thousand acres to work. He would be able to, at that time, finally put a number to his labor. A thousand.

But for right now – for six-year-old John – numbers didn't matter. The fields were simply endless and vast.

So he topped the stalks of tobacco, his arm moving rhythmically. It was boring, but it was life. Gave him time to think, time to dream. And always, always his rhythm accompanied him.

When he was done for the day he'd make his way back to the shack with the others, eat his meager food, and sit quietly in a corner until he fell asleep.

His magic didn't awaken until the first time he gripped the handle of a shovel.

▽

The fields needed to be worked aggressively. A day didn't go by that John wasn't expected to be doing something. The slaves always sang songs to the Lord on Sundays, and it seemed to be permitted for a time, but they'd get yelled at eventually and shamble out the door to start their day's work.

Then, in the midst of the monotony, came the day that John would never forget.

One dreadfully hot Sunday afternoon John saw another slave go to one knee, grabbing at his chest. John stood, mortified, as the man coughed and fell forward, his body hitting the dirt with a thud. John looked around. There was no one nearby. He didn't know if he could help, wasn't even sure if he was *supposed* to help. He dropped his pouch, ran over to the man, and knelt by him.

The man's eyes were wide, his breathing ragged. He'd dropped the shovel he'd been using. The tool lay next to him, its once silver blade rusted and covered in dirt.

"I go get da massa," John said quietly to the man.

The slave waved his hands. "No, no," he gasped. "I rather die out here. I rather be dead now." He reached up and gripped John's shirt. His nostrils flared. "You get away from here someday. You *do* somethin' with your life. Get educated. Don't belong to nobody. You unnastan' me?"

John nodded but didn't really know what the man meant. His words were scary, and carried a gravity that would take John years to truly appreciate.

"There's a whole world outside this place," the man said. "Yer young yet. You gotta . . . gotta get outta this if ya can." He put his face closer to John's. "Run," he said.

John didn't know where he'd run, and even if the

notion hadn't sounded crazy to him he knew it wasn't an option. Those that ran came back with teeth marks from the hounds, or bullet wounds, or worse.

"You know the song we sing," the dying man continued. "The one about followin' the stars. You take those words, boy, and you get da hell outta here. Maybe the Lord forsaken us. Don't forsake yourself. Get. Free."

The man's words continued to confuse John. His heart was pounding. The look on the man's face scared him: so desperate, so important, unlike anything he'd ever seen before. The man was gurgling now, choking on something. He spat up blood. He convulsed.

John was horrified.

The man didn't release his grip on John's shirt as he died so John had to pry his hands off, bending the dead fingers back like the gnarled roots of a tree.

John stood up and looked around. No one else was here. He wasn't quite sure what to do.

John had at least some notion of what burial was; it was in some of the songs that the slaves sung. He couldn't always understand the words, but there was a part about 'coverin' up da dead so da devil don't take 'em'. 'So the earth could have 'em back'. Something like that. He didn't know for sure.

He looked at the dead man; his eyes were still open but there was no breath coming from his mouth.

John picked up the shovel and began to scrape dirt up and over the man's feet. He started there because it was the least threatening part. Before he got too far along he had found his rhythm.

Scrape tap-a-tap. Scrape shuffle tap-a-tap. Scrape scrape shuffle shuffle tap-tap-a-tap.

Something happened.

John felt a shock run up his arms. Brown images

flashed in his head. He saw waves of dirt running over the ground. He could feel the cold beneath the surface, experienced the airlessness of being buried alive. He connected with worms and bugs and mice. He tasted dirt. His blood ran thick. He dropped the shovel and stumbled back from the dead man. The images stopped.

What I'm doin' is foolish, he thought. *I shouldn't be messin' with the Lord's things.*

He walked quickly to pick up his tobacco sack, his skin prickling in fear. Maybe he would tell someone about the man at day's end. Maybe he wouldn't. They'd know the man was gone either way. Maybe they'd think he escaped as he'd told John to do. He wondered what they would say.

It was most likely that no one would say a word.

For a while John stayed away from touching shovels.

But only for a while.

▽ CHAPTER 8 ▽

It was six long years later – around about the time of John's twelfth birthday - that a slave named Abel Black was purchased and brought to the plantation. Abel was large. He was at least three heads taller than John (who was getting mighty tall himself at this age) with bulging muscles and a broad back that seemed to defy the scars that were writ large upon it.

He didn't make much contact with anyone else and never sang along on Sundays or in the twilight hours when the work day was over. He slept outside instead of in the shack with everyone else. John didn't know why. Maybe Abel was allowed to break the rules; maybe he simply didn't care about the punishment.

He worked like no other slave that John had ever seen. The man was tireless, fervent, inspiring. He didn't talk, he only worked.

John found himself trailing behind Abel just to watch him. The man hoed, dug, harvested, and planted with such brutality that John wondered if the man was sane. He found himself both scared of and reverent of Abel at the same time. He would never in a million years have talked to him or even approached him.

But there was something more that captivated John; something in Abel's eyes. Or was it the way he moved. John had not only been careful around shovels for the past six years, he'd also ceased his rhythmic movements: his tongue clicks, his patterns of picking. Just in case what had happened near the dead man happened again. But Abel moved the way John had – with a recognizable rhythm - and it reminded him of who he had been.

Abel was too brutal to approach, though, too distant

and fearsome.

But one day John watched Abel pick a mouse up out of the field and run one giant finger across the tiny creature gently from head to tail. He was petting it. In that one simple act John felt the fear drain out of him.

That was the day John decided to talk to Abel.

▽

Night had fallen and John had gotten up the nerve. Abel was seated, leaning against the outside wall of the shack and staring off towards the setting sun. The shovel that Abel had been using that day was leaned up next to him, its handle worn smooth from where the huge man gripped it day in and day out.

John shuffled up, his bare feet making almost no noise against the dirt. Abel knew he was there anyway.

"I've been waiting for you," Abel said without breaking his westward gaze. His voice was deep and smooth, almost exactly what John would have expected.

John's heart nearly stopped. He'd faced the whip before and never been this nervous. "W-w-waitin'?" he squeaked. "For me?" He didn't know what else to say. He was stunned. "Uh . . . well . . . here I am." He felt idiotic, but it was too late to take it back.

Abel turned to look at John. Their eyes met and John couldn't hold the look so he focused on the shovel handle, staring at it as if his life depended on it. He waited.

"I seen ya out there," Abel said. "John, ain't it?"

"Yes," John said, not taking his eyes off the shovel. He felt Abel's appraising gaze upon him, never feeling nakeder than that moment, before or since.

"While you've been watchin' me, I've been watchin' you. Don't use a shovel much, do ya, John?"

John's blood froze. Abel suspected something. Somehow knew. There was something keenly perceptive about the man. John hadn't expected to feel so examined. He had only wanted to talk to someone else. Someone he looked up to.

"No," John replied.

"I got a guess why ya don't," Abel said.

John swallowed hard.

"Somethin' happened, didn't it, John?" Abel continued. "It's alright. You can tell me. I known others like you. You've got the Touch."

"How do you know?" John whispered.

"I can see it in the way you walk," the big slave said. "The way you move. Like you're holdin' back your movements. There's a rhythm in you that wants to break free, John, if you only let it. You mighta been scared up ta now, but we gotta make sure that you never fear your Touch again. It's too important."

John thought back to the day with the dying slave and how he'd felt when the earth had spoken to him. It had crawled inside of his body and mind and bared itself to him. "I'm cursed," he whispered.

"Naw," Abel said. "Far from it. You got somethin' special, John. Somethin' most men of power would kill for. But that's just the thing. Ya don't get the Touch by wantin' it, or killin' for it, and they'll never learn that. Follow me."

Abel stood and motioned for John to come.

$$\triangledown$$

The crickets chirped around John and Abel. The plants in the field blew in the gentle wind. A red-tinted moon hung high in the sky.

"The earth's got a rhythm," Abel said. "Listen

around you. Feel it in your toes. It pulses from the center, reaches out to us if we care ta listen. I ain't but thirty-five summers, but I've seen a few men like you, John, and I remember what they told me. It ain't much, but it might be enough to get you started down the right path. I wanna let you know not to be afraid, and that you need to embrace what God has given you."

"Do you have the Touch?" John asked cautiously.

"Me? No. But I try, I really do. I move with the rhythm that other slaves have taught me, tryin' to awaken the magic in myself. But, no. I'm just your guide, not your teacher. We can only do this if yer willin'. I can't guide you if you don't want my help. That's why I had to wait til you came to me. You had ta be ready, John."

John Henry stood there and he found he was yearning to be taught something, anything. Knowledge was something that he thirsted for. One time he'd found a book – a group of scribbles on multiple pieces of paper – and had become so fascinated with it that he'd lost a few night's sleep. He'd guarded it like a treasure until one day it had disappeared. He'd never found out where it had gone, but he ached for it sometimes still.

"Guide me," John said. "Please. I'm ready."

Abel nodded as if he'd known the answer was coming.

"You can connect with the world because of your Touch," he said. "The dirt'll listen to you if you know the right techniques. You'll be able to control the earth, to use it, to live through it, to understand it. All it takes is a little rhythm. Course, havin' a Focus helps, too." Abel indicated the shovel in John's hands.

John had forgotten he was even holding it.

"Everyone's got a Focus," Abel continued. "Mostly the person's Focus turns out to be a tool of the earth.

Makes sense. There's a connection there. The metal of that spade used to be deep under the ground, the wood of the handle was grown in the soil. You hold in your hands a thing made of the very earth itself. I know yer scared - yer young yet - but if you can harness the Touch early I'm told there ain't no limits to the powers you can wield.

"The mud will listen to you. The muck, the plants, maybe even the animals. But you need to experiment, train when no one's watchin'. When yer tired from a day of workin' the fields you can't rest, John. When the sky is dark that's gonna be your time to harness the Touch; you got no other options for now.

"It might not even be that hard for ya. Ya did it accidentally the first time, now we gonna try it on purpose."

Abel moved through the darkness, getting out of the way so that John would have room to try whatever it was he was supposed to try. The scars on the large man's back reflected the moonlight differently than the rest of his skin and John saw him, for an instant, like a great tiger from the stories.

John raised the shovel in front of him, not wanting to disappoint Abel. This had been the most anyone had talked to John in his entire life. It had been both exhilarating and terrifying listening to the words pour from Abel's mouth.

I won't disappoint him.

John took a shuffling step forward, trying to recreate what he had done near the dead man all those years ago. Abel had been right: John always moved with an intentional jerk, making sure he didn't accidentally create a rhythm like he had in the past. Now his limbs must have been angry at him, with him holding back his natural movement for so long, because he snagged his foot on a root and fell to the ground, the shovel clattering away along the hard-packed dirt.

Abel stood silently by and waited as John - his face burning with shame - retrieved the shovel and went to try again.

Shuffle step clank.

Nothing.

Shuffle step tap-a-tap.

Shuffle shuffle tap-a-tap step step clank.

Suddenly John smelled something like wet leaves and fur on the air. *No, probably not on the air,* he realized. *Inside of my own head.*

The scent faded as he stood still.

"Did it," he said, his voice cracking. "I . . . smelled somethin'. Like the earth. For jus' a bit."

"Are you afraid?" Abel asked quietly.

John took a few deep breaths to steady his nerves. "No," he said, but it was a lie. Abel had to have known it was a lie.

"Yer afraid," the big man said. "Won't work well when you're afraid. But when you brave up, I want you out here doin' this as often as you can. Don't get caught practicin', and don't give up. It's not everybody gets to have the Touch. But you do, John. Don't waste it."

Abel walked off without another word, leaving John alone in the cricketing night.

John did his best to follow Abel's instructions. He found safe places and times to practice. For those brief moments he became one with the world around him. The seasons slowly turned and still John practiced the Touch. As his rhythms became more complex – informed by the chirping bugs and movements he felt beneath the ground –

he could perform more and more interesting feats. His fear
slowly faded until he regarded himself not as cursed, but as
blessed.

After a year John's muscles were honed as much
from his work on the plantation as from his nightly
experimentation. The shovel he'd started with had long
since fallen apart, as well as the one after that and the one
after that. It was the only suspicious part of his training,
but it couldn't be helped.

After two years he began adding chops, thrusts, and
kicks to his routines. He had seen two great birds fighting
in the field one day and had felt the rhythm of their dance.
He had simply added it to his own.

John was practicing one chill night during his
sixteenth year on the plantation. He was feeling restless, his
own skin seeming too small for his body. He wanted to be
away; the dying slave's words still haunted him ten years
later. He felt that if he could only get powerful enough he
could flatten this place and be free.

Shuffle-shuffle-tap-tap-a-clang-clang-clickety-clang.
Tap-tap-tap-tap-a-clickety-clang. Kick-kick-shuffle-spin-clang-
clang-clang.

He forced his Touch through the shovel head and
suddenly the earth heaved. Great waves of dirt radiated out
around him. He lost his balance and fell crashing to the
ground. He looked up to watch the waves of earth flatten
rows of crops as they traveled away from him. He winced at
the rumbling sound the rolling earth made, his heart
pounding. When he stood up slowly and quietly he
appeared to be at the center of a crater. This disturbance
would certainly be noticed. The ground was bare in a
hundred foot circle, rocks that had been long-buried were
poking their ragged faces towards the sky. Bugs and mice
whose homes had been disturbed were fleeing along the

surface to find safety.

John felt that all-too-familiar mixture of exhilaration and fear. If he could get to the master's house and send out a ripple of earth like the one he'd just made . . .

He could bring the whole two-story place crashing down on its sleeping occupants. Maybe they would scream, cry out for help, the weight of the building crushing the life from them. They were weak, fat, lazy, stupid. He could escape the hounds who would never be able to run on the waving ground. He could . . . become a killer.

Thou shall not murder!

The thought came unbidden to John, and he knew in his soul that he was being foolish. For four years he had worked hard for the power to destroy the men that kept him, and now that he had it he knew he could never use it; could never go against the will of God. Even if most of the time he felt that God had abandoned him.

He stood as still as stone in the center of the crater and even though he knew he should have been running and hiding he began to laugh. His laughter was deep, his voice having become that of a man's a few years ago. It was loud laughter, coming from him in great peals as tears ran down his face.

He heard running footsteps approaching, knew the whip was probably coming for him but he couldn't stop laughing; the emotion was crippling.

John felt strong hands grip him and then he was being spun around.

It was Abel.

"Get outta here, John," the big man said. "God in heaven, what have you done? Never seen anything like it! Come with me, we gotta hide."

John didn't know what he'd done. He followed Abel to safety and slept fitfully, knowing he had the power to be

free of this place, but also completely certain that he lacked
the will to use it.

Abel counseled John that night, informing him that
he was unsure where to go from here. John had exceeded all
expectations and was now among the most powerfully gifted
slaves Abel had ever known. Freedom, though, was still an
elusive moral beast.

John could run, he was certain of that. He had been
practicing moving on top of the waves of earth, and also
learning how to put the earth back into place once he'd riled
it up. Mercifully, no one ever suspected his training and he
held the secret of his power close to himself.

And, as John eventually learned, time has a way of
solving a lot of problems if only you let it do its work.

John didn't end up having to kill anyone to be free.

One day in eighteen-sixty-three, when he was
seventeen years old, he was informed that, should he choose
to stay on the plantation, he would be paid because he was
now free. John was confused. Staying here didn't *seem* like
freedom to John, and by now, as a young man, he held
nothing in as high regard as freedom. He decided to go and
talk to Abel, but he knew what the big man would say.

The conversation was short. Indeed Abel had said
what John had anticipated he would. The two men struck
out together into the world with nothing but a small ration
of food, the clothes on their backs, and, of course, John's
shovel. They followed the words from the songs the slaves
had sung and soon John realized just how large America
really was.

Every new type of tree and animal he saw excited
him. The gathering of food didn't prove to be too difficult

and everything tasted so rich that John had had to spit out the first thing he'd eaten because there had been too much flavor. It took his mouth a few weeks to adjust to just how delicious the world was.

He practiced his magic at night until his shovel fell apart a few weeks later. He tried to mend it with Abel's help, but they didn't have the supplies to do so. He felt himself become rusty and frustrated over the next few days; could feel the Touch burning inside of him but couldn't let it free.

Now John was free in one way and bound in another. He had trouble sleeping and even briefly wondered if he had made the right decision.

Abel kept him in line, kept him going with promises that everything would turn out alright in the end.

$$\triangledown$$

One day the wind brought the scent of salt to John. Abel said they must be near the ocean: a huge body of water that you couldn't see across.

"You ever had ocean fish, John?" Abel asked.

"You know I haven't, Abel."

"You still got your shovel handle?"

"Yup."

Abel smiled. "Then get ready for somethin' special!"

The big man began walking towards the salty scent and John followed, the wind rippling his clothes. Eventually Abel's excitement overtook both men and they began to crash through underbrush and run beneath tall trees in their mad flight to the ocean. But then suddenly Abel stopped short.

A man with a rifle set to his shoulder was blocking the way. The man was squat, with small eyes and a ragged beard that hung to his belly.

Abel stood in front of John defensively.

"Hey, boys," the man with small eyes said, not lowering his rifle. "Just where da hell d'ya think yer goin'?"

"If this's yer land I'm sorry," Abel said carefully. "We're just passin' through, makin' our way north until we can find work."

The man with small eyes tongued his teeth. "I might have work for ya," he said, clicking a dangerous part of his gun. "Why don'tcha come with me, no trouble."

John looked at Abel. The older, larger man was stoic, his strong brow glistening with sweat, his eyes locked with the other man's.

They were led northwest at gunpoint. None of this sat right in the pit of John's stomach. Without his shovel he was mostly defenseless. He knew Abel was frustrated, too, and probably working on how to get out of this. John had no clue what the outcome would be, but he knew it wouldn't be good.

He had no idea just how bad it was going to be.

▽ CHAPTER 9 ▽

"There's bad men in this world, Whistler," John said.

The fire was burning orange on John's taut black face and Whistler saw a haunted look in his eyes for the first time during the telling of his story.

"We can stop talkin' for tonight if ya want," Whistler said gently. "Look, the angel's sleepin', and it's quiet out here." He felt his leg and arm wounds pulling, starting to scab.

"Nah," John said. "Ya gotta hear what I got to say. Let the angel rest and let's talk. It's good for me to get this off my chest after all these years." John sighed. "Well, anyway, Abel and I tasted freedom, Whistler. It might be somethin' you take for granted."

"Well-"

"I don't mean to accuse," John said, holding up his hands. "I just mean to speak the truth. Those few days - the ones where we traveled from our first slavery unwittingly towards our second - were the first great ones I had ever had." John looked off into the dark distance, his eyes glittering in the firelight. "Abel and I were fast friends at this point, and what ya gotta understand, Whistler, is that we had never talked a lot on the plantation. There wasn't a need. The conversations I just now recounted for ya were some of the only ones we ever had. We had a kinship born on the plantation, ya see. So it worried me when our talkin' went from infrequent to never. What ya gotta understand about the next part, and what I might not portray properly in my tellin', is how much it hurt to feel like I was losin' my friend. And that's what it felt like in this next part. Losin' my freedom didn't hurt half as much as losin' my friend."

The small-eyed man with the rifle had taken Abel and John to some manner of local authority, insisted that they had been breaking the law, and had said they'd needed to be arrested. The whole transaction had been a sham and everyone involved had known it, but that hadn't stopped it from happening.

John now had shackles from wrist to wrist and ankle to ankle. He and other dirty, silent men moved in a large gang, bound together with a long chain that clanked as they walked.

The work that the men in John's prison gang did got more disgusting with each passing day. At first it had been picking fresh corpses: taking the clothes, weapons, and valuables off of men recently dead, leaving them stripped and bare.

As time had dragged on, however, the corpses they found were more and more decayed: faces falling off, limbs separating when the shirt was pulled from the torso, hair blown away, worms in the sockets. John became detached, withdrawn. He worked silently in his shackles, the other men around him doing the same. Occasionally he tried to talk to Abel, but the large man never responded and soon John became frustrated. He'd been trying to draw hope from Abel, but, just when he needed him most, the man seemed a different person entirely.

Today they were picking the same type of decaying corpses John had become used to of late.

John reached his large hands down to pry the ring from a spindly finger, twisting it off as gently as he could. He could feel the bones trying to separate, the flesh trying to tear. He prayed that the finger wouldn't come off.

Mercifully, the ring came off this dead man's finger without the finger attached. John looked at the ring for a moment and then put it into his burlap sack. It clanked against the other jewelry, buttons, and bullets that he had already collected that day.

'Collecting the useful bits of quickly-forgotten men who had served some purpose and then been thrown away.' That would have been John's description of the job.

War, he had decided one day not too long ago, seemed a lot like slavery.

It had been a shocking thought.

His life on the plantation had been hard, but these men seemed no better off. All of their corpses were gaunt, weak, malnourished. These men hadn't needed to be strong to do their job, they had just needed to be kept alive long enough so that they could die at the right moment.

John and the other prisoners had traveled from battlefield to battlefield under the sickening gaze of power-eyed men with guns. Their shackles were never removed, even when they were working.

"The men are whisperin' that we're gonna be stayin' here awhile." The voice startled John. It was Abel. This was the first sentence he had spoken to John since their abduction. His eyes were dark, his shoulders slumped.

"Whaddya mean stayin'?" John asked.

"Big battlefield up north a few miles. Say there's buildings up there. Housing. For us. We gonna be in this life a long time."

Abel had been right.

The shack where John was kept now was even smaller than the one on the plantation had been, and his shackles were still never removed. He had been living with them on for almost two months straight. He felt like the bands of iron were beginning to choke the life from him. He started having nightmares. His body and mind were withering away.

He had personally picked at least a thousand corpses by now and couldn't image how many more lay scattered about the plains and the woods of the region. He had noticed at least three other prison gangs working the same area.

Day in and day out the men picked corpses - and then, eventually, skeletons - under the hot sun. The smell barely bothered John anymore. He struggled to keep his hope alive, to trust that Abel or someone, anyone - would make everything right again.

He had tasted freedom so very briefly, and it had been so sweet and so overpowering that he tried to shut the memory away. He knew remembering that sensation right now would be torture so he willed his mind to stillness.

He never saw Abel anymore. The man was a ghost, large though he was.

John felt that he had failed; that he had let his only friend down somehow. Maybe the only friend he'd ever had in his life. Maybe the only one he'd ever have.

One particularly chill night, when the bugs that incessantly plagued the battlefield were too numbed to fly, John found himself working before the sun had come up, forced out into the field of death by his masters. His cold fingers fumbled for other cold fingers. He tore buttons free from thread that snapped easily. He took bloodied lockets with pictures of family inside, undelivered letters, socks, boots, everything.

There was no way to get a rhythm going with this type of work. It was too grotesque, too disgusting. And so the Touch was no use here. There didn't seem to be any escape. They never buried anybody so John had never been given a shovel. He had scanned the camp for other tools, but there were none that he could find.

He'd had hope at first, but that had slowly dwindled. Without Abel, John lacked the will to bring himself to action.

But still he kept-

"We're gettin' out," Abel said, startling John. He hadn't even know the large man was there.

"When?" John asked, still bent over the corpse he was picking. "How?"

"You'll know," Abel said. "Be ready, John Henry. We're gettin' out. And . . . if you gotta kill a few of these monsters on the way, God'll forgive you. Just this once."

▽ CHAPTER 10 ▽

Weeks passed and there was no sign of anything changing. Abel's words didn't seem to be coming true. John's despair sank back in. There were rumors that the prison gang was done at this place. John couldn't stand the thought of being herded somewhere else, but he knew resistance probably meant death and John Henry wasn't ready to die. Not yet.

He'd seen other prisoners shot. He had been *meant* to see them get shot.

John sat against the wall of his shack on this night, which was so much like many other nights. He'd stared at the wall for hours until he must have fallen asleep. He awoke and something knocked hard against his door. He sat up, his limbs aching from too much work and too little food.

Now he crawled to the door and pulled it open slowly. An object lay on the ground, glistening in the moonlight.

A shovel.

John snatched the tool quickly and scurried back into his shack.

Abel.

John could barely stand in the shack, but he did so now, his head bent so that it didn't scrape the rough wooden top. He held the shovel in two hands, the implement feeling weird after a quarter-year of not holding one.

He knew that he could do now what he hadn't been able to bring himself to do on the plantation. He would kill any man that stood in his way. Abel had said to.

So John reached inside himself and tried to find the Touch. It was like searching for a mouse among weeds.

John felt rusty, could almost taste iron in his mouth. He concentrated. John felt a stir inside and tried to harness it so he could begin his rhythm. He began to tap the spade on the chain that ran between his ankles.

Tap tap tap tap.

His power exploded through his shovel and shattered the chain, the links flying through the air, one of them shooting across his arm, tearing the skin. The whole thing made an awful racket.

No stopping now.

He began to hear shouts and commotion from outside his shack. Gunshots pierced the air. He heard more than one desperate yell.

John couldn't figure out how to touch his wrist shackles with the shovel tip, and he didn't have time to puzzle it out. He had to act. He burst from the shack into a night that was filled with chaos. Shadows of men ran frantically through the darkness, tripping, yelling, dying, screaming. The prisoners were putting up an admirable resistance.

But there was only one man that John truly cared about.

He looked around until he saw Abel's massive outline against the moonlit sky. Three gray men with rifles closed on him. John assumed they were out of bullets or they surely would have shot him. Abel was big, but he must have been as weakened as John; there was no way he could fight three men alone, especially in shackles and they with weapons.

John ran through the darkness, his shovel gripped tightly in aching hands. He began tapping and shuffling along the way, trying to recreate the waves of earth that he had done accidentally that night on the plantation.

Tap tap shuffle clank. Tap tap tap tap. Tap tap tap

shuffle tap-

BLAM!

Something hit him in the leg and he was spun sideways. He almost lost his grip on the shovel. The pain in his leg was incredible, dull and sharp all at the same time. A shadowed man with a rifle approached John as the three others moved even closer to Abel.

"Lay down your weapon!" the gray rifleman yelled.

But John felt the Touch wanting to burst free. He'd come so close to completing the pattern. He saw hatred in the gray man's eyes. *No,* he thought. *Not just hatred. Fear. I have the power here.* So John brought the shovel down swiftly to complete what he had started and just as it touched the ground he let his power free, felt it flow down his arm and into the handle and-

BLAM!

Something exploded in his side and John Henry sank to his knees, gasping.

The man with the rifle stood over him, bayonet held to John's neck. "Get up, boy," he said. "Show's over."

John heard Abel cry out and then everything became silent.

▽

John sat in a new cell in near darkness, his wrists and ankles shackled together and to each other and to the wall. *They don't want me gettin' away again.* His back and shoulders screamed with pain. He couldn't move very far so he had spent most of the past three days sitting on the hard floor, leaning against the hard wall, feeling the bullets that were still in his leg and side.

He set his jaw and waited patiently. He hadn't gotten anything to eat or drink since his escape attempt.

His ragged clothes were even filthier than usual, and he didn't hear any other voices. They'd put him away. Maybe for good.

He was almost certain - if they ever even came to let him out - that they would hang him for his crime. There was no fairness here. He didn't expect justice anymore. By now, at age eighteen, John Henry was nearly beaten, body and mind. He clung now to the smallest shred of hope, a wispy lock of goodness.

The door opened and light streamed in.

John shielded his eyes, his chains jangling as he did so.

A man that John did not recognize entered the small cell.

He was white and old with small bagged eyes and a puffy, graying beard. He walked with the aid of a cane. He limped in, dignified, unafraid of John. Maybe he should have been. They gray man had been afraid of John's power and strength. John had seen it in his eyes. But John did not see the same thing in this man's eyes.

The man knelt, a brief flash of pain on his face. He used his cane to guide himself to the ground where he ended up sitting. It was queer behavior and John immediately knew something was different here. Other men had always tried to tower over him, trying to prove their dominance, but this man had lowered himself almost immediately upon entering.

"Oh," the man said, laughing. "It'll be hard gettin' up again."

John sat silently, not quite knowing what to do.

"Name's Huntington. Collis Huntington." The man's voice was kind and almost as deep as John's. Collis took off his hat and began to fan his face with it. "My lord it's hot in here."

John leaned back against the wall. He wondered if this was some kind of trick. Didn't seem to make sense that it would be, but everything about this situation was strange.

"I'm here with an offer for you."

John waited, content with his own silence for the time being.

"Yes, well, I can see you're not much on talkin' right now," Collis continued. "I don't blame you. I assure you I come in good faith, Mr. Henry. Truth of the matter is, I don't come across a man like you very often. Word has come to me about, ah, what you can do. Or what you were *trying* to do with the shovel. The wardens thought it was hilarious, watching you try to defend yourself using only a shovel. They're idiots. They don't really understand. But I do. Ya see, I'm always looking for men like you. I'm offering employment, Mr. Henry."

"You need a man who can pick a good corpse?" John asked grimly.

Collis ran his hand over his beard. "You know that's not what I mean, Mr. Henry. I'm in charge of railroad expansion projects and many of those railroads require tunnels. Sometimes it takes a thousand men several years to build the tunnels I need. If I want to stay competitive I need to have advantages. In exchange for your help clearing the earth I'll pay you fairly."

John was silent once more.

"Still being difficult," Collis said. "I'm offering you freedom. I know they've treated you like an animal here. It's wrong, Mr. Henry, and I aim to see it fixed. Although, perhaps I'm not being fair if I don't tell you everything. My offer isn't ironclad. There's inherent risk in it, Mr. Henry. You see, I've worked with three men like you during my time on the railroads. All of them have met grizzly ends. So know this: if you come and work for me you will have freedom of one kind and bondage of another."

"I already got plenty of bondage."

Collis paused, leaned back and closed the door, shutting out the light and ushering in darkness. He lowered his voice and said, "Are you familiar with demons, Mr. Henry?"

Now that peaked John Henry's interest something fierce. He felt the strangeness of this conversation begin to overtake his obstinacy.

"I already got demons, too," he said, but not with much conviction.

"I understand," Collis said. "I want you to know that I don't support slavery. I think it's a vile, disgusting practice. So, no, I don't mean demons as in the white demons that surround you, treating you and people like you as less than men. No. I mean *demons*."

John's eyes had adjusted to the new darkness. He saw Collis's face: deadly serious. "I'm listenin'," he said quietly.

"They take all forms," Collis continued. "They can be creatures of grotesque build. Sometimes they inhabit machines, turning a hunk of metal into a thing almost alive. And sometimes they are men. It's very hard to tell a demon from a man sometimes, Mr. Henry. Lord knows I don't have the power to do it. But demons are drawn to men such as yourself, eventually. Once you start using your powers regularly, they will feel you and know you. So I'm warnin' ya. I can get you out of here if you want to come work for me, but it'll be a mixture of glory and danger that you walk into."

The fact that this might be a joke still played around the edges of John's mind, but his gut told him that it wasn't. This was real. A man like Collis Huntington - a man whose every detail spoke of great care and serious thought - didn't make jokes.

And so, as his emotions fought within him, John Henry chose his fate.

"I wanna be away from here," he said. "Don't care where it is, don't care what I'm doin'. Don't care if a hundred demons come and gut me. Don't wanna be here."

"Excellent," Collis said. He put his hat back on his bald head, gripped his cane and tried to push himself up off the ground. It was a struggle for him, but he managed it. He smoothed his fine pants, vest, and overcoat. "You'll be free within the hour, Mr. Henry. You in a condition to ride?"

"I can do it," he said.

Collis smiled. "Confidence from a man who looks like Hell itself has run over him. I like it." He shook his head. "Your strength has been wasted here, Mr. Henry. You belong with my men. I'll see you patched up and out of here."

Collis turned to go and John rose as best he could. He felt his throat tighten. He didn't know if he was in a position to bargain, but he wasn't about to leave this place without Abel. "I got a favor ta ask of ya."

"Oh?" Collis said.

"A friend of mine," John said. "Abel Black. Can ya free him too?"

"Can he do what you do?"

"No, sir. But he helped me become what I am. And he's the hardest workin' man I ever seen."

"If that's the case I'll free him, too."

"Thank you," John said. "Thank you, sir."

"You help build me a tunnel like I know you can, Mr. Henry, and I'll be the one thanking you."

▽ CHAPTER 11 ▽

John Henry couldn't have been happier. When he and Abel arrived at the Big Bend Tunnel it was nothing but a mountain that hadn't known a spike. After John and a thousand other men sweat on it for a while, it was starting to look like a train might actually be able to go through it.

The work camp was noisy, bustling, never anything like the plantation and certainly nothing like the prison camp. There had been jokes and laughter at the other places John had been, but never had it felt so rich and real.

John saw Abel come alive in this place. If John had thought the man was a hard worker on the plantation, he saw a new side of him that he hadn't known existed. Abel was a beast with a hammer. Driving spikes was a new task for both of the men, but Abel adapted the quickest. John watched him work and tried to mimic him as best he could, but the only way he could get close to surpassing the man's productivity was by using the Touch.

He'd had to relearn parts of it, of course. A hammer wasn't a shovel and the power flowed differently. He'd worked on the timing and rhythms. They were different for the hammer, shorter and more powerful. The ringing of steel on steel permeated the air from sunup to sundown, and John's hammer was always a part of it.

It took him two months to figure out the timing he needed in order to transfer his magic from his body, to the hammer, to the spike, to the earth all in the blink of an eye as the blow fell. The first time it had happened he'd nearly fallen over as his spike sank easily into the ground. He'd stood up, blinking with wonder as rock crumbled away like dust before him.

He'd learned to feel the weakest paths through the

rock, making his routes the most efficient ones in the whole company.

Even so, it was slow going, digging a hole through a mountain.

The rock didn't want to be moved. John broke through its resistance as he drove his spike into it over and over, chipping off chunks that were then hauled away by the pickers to be crushed up for bed under rail lines that needed to be laid.

This wasn't picking tobacco, or picking corpses. This was a place where John felt at home. And he laid his whole back into it.

"So ya got yer friend back," Whistler said to John.

"For a time," John agreed. "But Collis had been right about demons. He probably had a hard job before he came to rescue me, figurin' out the worth of my productivity versus the price of drawin' demons to his rail lines. I think in the end he chose right. But I'll let you be the judge of that."

▽ CHAPTER 12 ▽

Abel sat down next to John and sighed. It was a sound that John hadn't heard from the man in the year they'd been here on the Big Bend Tunnel.

"You're usin' the Touch full on now, aren't ya?" Abel asked.

"Yeah," John said.

"I can tell," Abel replied. "You beat me today, John. Startin' to make a name for yourself 'round here."

"Not a contest, Abel. You told me that."

Abel laughed. "Don't matter much what I say in a group of a thousand men."

"It does," John said. "If I dug farther than you today it's just my Touch doin' it." John looked around. "You . . . you seen any demons?" he whispered.

"None that I know of since the last time you asked me. I've seen just good men workin' hard and gettin' paid and eatin' food. It's enough to make my heart swell out of my chest. I got a feelin' Collis is more superstitious than he lets on. These demons might not be real. I never seen no sign of anything since we left the prison gang. Your mind ain't settled down since nothin's been happenin'?"

"It's always in the back of my mind," John admitted, a little ashamed. He'd been brought up believing a mixture of folklore and the Bible. He knew in his heart that most of it wasn't real, but Collis had been straightforward about it. And what's more, John believed that Collis had truly meant every word.

"You put too much weight on Collis's words. He's just a man like the rest of us. This idea of demons he's laid in your head, I don't know 'bout it. I think we've already met our devils John, and I think we already beat 'em."

"You're prolly right. But Collis . . ."

"Just cuz he's convinced don't mean you gotta be. Look, John, I believe in God but I don't guess I'm gonna see him walkin' around down here by me."

"Well, alright," John said. "Just keep your eyes open for me, would ya?"

"I always do," Abel said. "I always do."

The next day, three men showed up with a giant machine in tow.

▽

The three men strode into camp right in the middle of the work day and caused everyone to slow down and stare. They were plain enough men, all in faded clothing with suntanned faces, but what followed behind them was catching the eyes of every man on the Big Bend Tunnel, including John's and Abel's.

It was a machine that belched and jerked along the ground, moving on long limbs that made it resemble a five-legged spider. It had a spiraling protrusion that stuck out the front, threatening to unbalance its bulky body. It gleamed silver in the noonday sun.

One of the men pulled a lever and the machine stopped and quieted itself.

"Who's in charge of this here operation?" one of the men asked.

"Collis Huntington," a tunnel worker answered. He took his hat off and wiped his brow with a rag.

"Somebody fetch him," the man said.

"He prolly knows yer here. I'm sure ya woke half the county with that contraption!" one of the rail layers joked. The tunnel workers laughed, but the men with the machine didn't; they looked at each other as if trying to decide what to do.

Silence fell over the area for the first time John could remember since being here. His heart started to beat too fast. One of the tunnel workers raced off to locate Collis and soon the older man came puffing into camp, walking hurriedly, his cane clicking a fast rhythm.

"Who's the best digger here?" one of the three machine men yelled to Collis as soon as he was within earshot.

John stood perfectly still. He knew his name would be mentioned any moment.

And certainly it was.

John approached the men cautiously, and at the same time he studied the machine they had brought with them. It was unlike anything he had ever seen. A great many sinister belts and gears adorned it.

"Who are you?" Collis asked the men with the machine.

"We're representatives of the Gast Corporation," one of them replied. "They sent us out here with an offer for you, Mr. Huntington. We've been long watching your work and we know that when it comes down to it you're a man who values deadlines. And this rail tunnel is almost overdue."

Another one of the men patted the side of the machine. "What we got here is the new Gast Co. steam drill model 002. Just put 'em into manufacturing a few months back. Our boss sent us out here to show you the capability of this beauty. It's affordable, never sleeps, and - best of all - never asks for a pay raise."

The third man stepped forward. "Of course, for

perspective, we'll let it race your strongest man." He looked
at John. "That you?"

John nodded. "I guess so," he said. Something was
tingling in John's hands and arms; the Touch wanted to
break free right at this very moment. He held it back.

"Then I'm sorry for ya, son. If your boss agrees to
this you got a lickin' comin' in the mornin'."

Collis pulled John aside while the crowd of men
around them looked on silently.

"What do you think?" Collis whispered.

John appraised the machine. "I'll do whatever you
ask me to do, sir."

"Now I'm not too keen on machines like this," Collis
said. "But the revolution's comin'. Other rail lines are usin'
'em. If I can't keep up I can't do business. I've resisted
other offers, but I can't do that forever. I'm takin' heat on
all sides. Investors tellin' me I'm too old-fashioned. But I'll
tell you what, Mr. Henry. You've done fine work for me
here, just as I knew you could. You beat that thing and I'll
send these men packin' and we can get back to work here."

"I didn't understand the stakes," John said to
Whistler. "But Abel . . . Abel set me right."

▽ CHAPTER 13 ▽

It was late, the sun just disappearing. John was walking over the grounds that he had come to know for the past year. The world was quiet even though a thousand men slumbered nearby. Tonight John walked, thinking about the contest that Collis had volunteered him for tomorrow.

A race against the machine.

He walked towards the machine now. It was resting just a few feet away from the railroad tracks. He wanted to get a better look at it, see what he was up against. As he approached it he realized that it was more intricate than he had first noticed. Aside from the usual machine parts he noticed that designs had been etched into its surface. He hadn't seen them by the light of day, but now subtle shadows were throwing them into view. There was something alien about the symbols that made John's hair stand on end. As he walked around the side of the machine he was frightened to see the three men leaning against it and whispering softly to one another.

They looked up at John in eerie unison, the twilight casting their faces in soft shadow. Their eyes seemed different now, not quite focused forward but just slightly off to opposite sides. One man's teeth, now that he was smiling, were a little bit too long, the roots too visible.

Demons.

John knew it instinctively. They looked like men but they weren't. Why hadn't John noticed before? Hadn't Collis seen it when he had talked to them? No. In the light they had looked normal, but in this near-darkness . . .

"John Henry, isn't it?" one of the demons said, taking the cigarette from between its lips.

"Yeah," John said. He wished suddenly that he had a

hammer. Or two.

"Funny how things work," another demon said. "We were just talking about coming to find you, but here you are. Saved us the walk. How thoughtful of you."

"What'd ya wanna see me 'bout?" John asked. He took a step backwards.

"I think he knows," the third demon said. It had a long mustache that drooped over part of its mouth, obscuring John's view of it.

"Yeah," said the first. "Look at his eyes. He sees what we are." It held up a hand. The fingers looked long. "Listen, John. I know what you must think. Good and evil and all that. Believe me when I tell you that it's never so simple."

The second demon spoke. "However, what we wanted to talk to ya about *is* simple." He glanced at his compatriots, as if checking to make sure what he was about to say was permissible. "We wanted to let you know not to win the contest tomorrow."

"Why?" John asked.

"Our motives are our own," the third demon said. "We need our machine to do well out there. Think of it as a business proposition if you must. It costs you nothing to lose. Lose and we'll be on our way. It's easy. Slick and shiny like a brand new shipment of spikes."

"What makes ya think I care about the contest?" John asked.

"The fact that you asked that question!" the first demon said, pointing and chuckling. "If you didn't care you woulda said 'Okey Dokey' and we'd be done talkin' now. But you've got standards, yes sir. You must forget them for now, John. And you must lose the contest." The demon patted the side of the machine. It issued a hollow clank. "Think of our metal friend, here. He's got feelings too, ya know?"

John stood silent for a moment.

"He's thinking it over," the first demon said.

"He knows what's at stake," said the second.

"We'll kill your friend Abel if you win," the third blurted out.

The other two glared at the third demon, their eyes thin slits.

"Whaaat?" the third demon hissed. "He makes me nervous! Don't he make you nervous?"

The first demon nodded. "He's got that look about him. Be mighty fine in our ranks, but I doubt that'll happen."

"Alright," John said, mostly so they would stop running their mouths. "I'll lose the contest."

"That's more like it," the first demon said.

"And now that you've seen us for what we are," the second demon said, "don't alert Collis. That'll have a similar outcome to winning the contest."

"Yes, that's right," the third demon said. "We'll see you in the morning, John. Look sluggish out there now!"

They turned their heads back to how they were when John had first come upon them and so he took his leave, retreating quickly through the night.

$$\triangledown$$

"I thought somethin' was strange when they showed up," Abel said after John had told him the tale. He was sitting against the cold rock of the mountain like he always did; outside, away from the other men, his hammer next to him. "But demons. Are you sure?"

"Sure as I've ever been about anything."

Abel whistled low. "Sorry, John. Demons. Sorry

that I tried to talk you out of believin'.

"It's alright," John said. "Look, Abel . . . when I lose . . . well, I think you should be away from here anyway."

Abel tensed. "Oh, I ain't runnin', and you ain't losin'," Abel said. "If I run they'll likely just find someone else to take it out on. No, I'll pay the price for this if I have to. Huh. Demons. Now that I know they're real it makes me wonder. They coulda been anywhere. Anytime. On the plantations. On the road. In the jail. You sure they're demons and not just bad men? There's probably room for both in this world, ya know."

"Yeah. I'm sure. If you ever trusted me at all, trust me now. Look, Abel, I'm gonna lose. It don't cost me nothin'."

"Remember those are *their* words, John. Don't talk like that. It brings you low. It brings all of us low."

John hung his head. "I don't see another way out. I wish I wasn't caught up in this. But Collis warned me it was possible. I shoulda listened. Never come. Never dragged us both here."

Abel shook his head. "You saved us, John Henry. I was as good as gone on that prison gang. I couldn't believe that the Lord would let me down the way he did. I was too blind to see that He'd sent you to save me."

John felt his face burn hot. The sentiment meant a lot coming from Abel.

Abel looked up at the stars for a long moment. "A man ain't nothin' but a man," he said finally. He looked back at John. "But a man always has the chance to do his best." He ran his left hand over his rippling right arm. "You see this?" he asked.

John nodded.

"They make us this way. They work us 'til we die. And now they try to *replace us*. Well, I got too much *pride* for that, John. I believe that men should work hard, *deserve* to work hard. We can't control our freedom, can't control our own lives, can't control anything . . . but we can always work. Ain't nobody gonna stop us from doin' that. Good or bad, they all want work." Abel stood up, towering in the darkness. "You beat that machine, John," he said, putting a finger against John's chest. "You beat it back to Hell where it came from. You use everything you got from God and you show those demons that we can't be *bullied*. For me and the thousand men that look up to you, you show 'em that we're stronger than anything they could imagine!" He sat back down and looked up at the stars again. "And you let me deal with payin' the price."

▽ CHAPTER 14 ▽

The morning was cool. John felt the breeze slide over his skin attempting to wake him up. He hadn't slept well, having stayed up most of the night thinking about what Abel had said to him.

He got out of his cot and tore into a hunk of his rations, eating hard bread and dried meat thoughtlessly while his brain attempted to fire.

Maybe I couldn't win even if I wanted to, he thought. His arms felt heavy, like someone had attached lead weights to his wrists.

The camp was bustling even more than usual, men shouting and moving about. They knew what was coming. Entertainment of this caliber was few and far between. There was a positive energy in the air that couldn't quite touch John. He knew now after Abel's speech that a lot of the workers probably felt the same way. He'd not known pride could be so strong.

But doesn't pride come before the fall?

He glanced over at his hammer. The head was marred from contact with countless thousands of spikes, the handle polished to a shine by his sweaty palms. It was a beautiful thing.

He grabbed hold of it and tapped it twice on the ground, sending a wave of magic below, feeling around him. He felt feet against the earth, could tell the size of each man's shoes and in some cases what condition the footwear was in. He felt every tiny living thing writhing beneath him. He felt the rails running smooth and even on top of their gravel and boards, and he felt them disappear into the tunnels that he and the men had dug for the past year.

And he felt the machine.

Its five feet were oddly shaped and stood out against everything else, evil imprints on an otherwise beautiful stretch of earth.

John cut the connection and exited his tent to cheers. The men had been waiting for him. More than a few slapped him on the back as John made his way to the contest site, his hammer held weakly in his left hand. He was still sagging despite the morning's greetings.

He stopped near the well and hauled the bucket up, taking several drinks from the dipper while men talked at him. He turned and shook hands with a few men, all the while looking for Abel. He didn't find him, but that didn't mean anything. John wasn't even sure if Abel would show up to watch the contest if it meant being crammed into the middle of a crowd.

John located the machine near the mountainside that he and it would be digging through. He wrestled with decisions that he didn't want to make. What would it really mean to lose? It would be intangible; something that wouldn't affect anybody.

Or am I just making excuses for Abel's sake?

John was near the machine now. Collis was there along with the three demons. John took a deep breath and stepped forward.

"John," Collis said, turning and waving in greeting. "You ready?"

John nodded.

"Alright. Stakes are simple," Collis said, turning to the demons. "Ya got an hour to dig the longest tunnel. If your machine here beats my man you'll have your contract and I'll use these machines on my next line. If not . . ."

"Oh, sir," the mustached demon said, its eyes dancing towards John, "let's not talk about the other outcome." It laughed.

The crowd was hunched in close as John stood facing the side of the mountain, the digging machine just a few feet away. John looked at the rock and stamped his feet, using the rhythm to peek into the stone. He could see the path: the places where the rock was weakest. It would be easy to annihilate these demons and their machine.

But he felt like the price of victory was too much, no matter what Abel had said. He banished his Touch.

There was no time to think anymore. Collis brought his hand down and the machine ground to life. John could hear the oil squelching in it, hear its belts moving. And then the machine's bit hit the mountain with a grinding sound loud enough to drown out the nervous voices of the thousand gathered men.

John took his spike and his hammer and got to work. The first clank of his hammer was met with cheers from the men behind. The spike drove deep into the rock, cracking it, spidery veins radiating out. One more strike and stone was already crumbling away in great chunks that John shoved aside to make way for his next hit.

But he didn't have a rhythm. His magic was stored up inside of him. He would not let it out this day. He cursed his selfishness, but he couldn't help it. Abel meant too much to him. He was the man that had shown John that he could be more than just a slave.

The men cheered John on as the machine whirred and clanked, the three demons running around it pushing and pulling various levers, urging it along. Slowly, slowly it disappeared into the face of the mountain, stone chunks flying and marking its path. John was out of the sun now, too, but just by a few inches. The coolness of the earth surrounded him on all sides, the cheers of the men muffled in the small space.

John was stalling. Abel had told him to win. He

wanted to lose. He worked at the stone without much
conviction. A quick shuffle of his feet let him feel that the
machine was indeed ahead of him. His heart seized at the
thought, emotion welling inside. The cheers of the men
were flagging. John felt the energy of the moment fade.
Something inside of him hurt.

It *was* tangible. The men behind him were in pain.
Seeing him lose would be too much. Something would die
here today if he lost. Something more than just Abel; the
spirit of men who believed in themselves. John would do a
disservice to all those who had worked and toiled and sweat
and died here.

He had almost convinced himself there was nothing
at stake. Almost. He felt his heart beating stronger in his
chest. Abel was right: John couldn't lose to these demons
no matter what the price. *Is there even enough time left to
win?* He felt the machine's progress. For a moment he felt
that everything was lost. The hammer slipped from his
hand and clanked to the ground. He heard someone gasp
outside.

John turned and walked out of his tunnel. He
brushed the dust from his overalls. The sun shone hot on
John Henry then, and he felt a thousand pairs of eyes on
him. Men gripped their hats in tight fists, mouths open in
anticipation.

John surveyed the crowd.

"I'm gonna need a second hammer," he said.

Shouts of joy erupted as twenty hammers worked
their up into the hands of the men in the front. John
selected the finest one and made his way back inside the
tunnel where he picked up his own hammer again. Now he
held one hammer over each shoulder. He took another
spike out of his pocket and drove it into the rock in front of
him. Now there were two in the wall.

Clank. Clank-a-clank. Clank-clank-shuffle-clank.

He let the Touch burst free. The rock gave way as if it were clay. Pulverized stone drifted to the ground. John juggled both hammers and both spikes, becoming a whirlwind of destruction inside the mountain. He couldn't see anything but red dust and he couldn't hear anything but clanking and crunching.

He was connected to the earth in a way he had never been before or since, but something was driving him that was greater than himself. He worked tirelessly. He ignored his burning muscles, the dust in his lungs, the sweat in his eyes.

There was no time to stop, not even for a moment.

John felt around him, sensed the whole area, knew every crevice. He felt the cold of the stone, the vibration of the spikes, the whirling heads of his twin hammers. He felt the machine, now with only a slight lead, but time was ticking away.

John burned for clean breath. He reached within himself and drew the entirety of his past into each strike.

CLANK! Seventeen years spent as a slave.

CLANG! Arrested unfairly.

CLANK! Digging through the dead.

CLANG! Learning from Abel what it meant to be a man.

CLANK! Demons.

He heard the chanting from outside. "IRON JOHN! IRON JOHN! IRON JOHN!"

He lost himself in time.

CLANG! The Touch was burning alive in him, his magic bursting at the seams, threatening to rip him to shreds.

CLANK! For all the injustice.

CLANG! For all the pain in the world.

CLANK! For the friend he would lose this day.

One last burst with both hammer heads brought him to the end of the competition.

He heard Collis yell that it was time to stop, and heard the cheers of the men who knew he had won.

John staggered out from his tunnel, fell to both knees, and then collapsed onto the ground, a beam of sunlight marking the place where he lay.

△ PART 3: FIRE △

△ CHAPTER 15 △

Whistler found his mouth hanging open. "Did ya win?" he whispered.

John nodded. "Yeah," he said. "But it cost me. I got sick for a long time. Lost the Touch for a good while. And the demons killed Abel as they'd said they would. Even killed a lot of other men on the tunnel before they ran with their tails 'tween their legs. Guess they were powerful mad."

"Probably an understatement," the angel said. He was awake again and looked a bit better, the color returning to his face, the golden blood dry. He'd caught the end of John's story. "But what brings you out here after all of that?"

"When I got well enough to walk again," John said, "I vowed that I would relearn what I had lost and come after the demons and their machine. I got word it was bein' used on the Rock Island Railroad layin' the Kansas lines. The tracks ain't but twenty miles southwest of here. Was on my way, then I ran into you."

"Southwest?" the angel asked. He looked at Whistler, turning his head on his too-long neck. "The course we're on leads us exactly in that direction. Fate."

"We'll be safer with you around," Whistler said to John.

"Love ta travel together," John said. "I'd warn ya what yer in for, but you've already seen a bit of it." John gazed at the angel for a moment. "Look, I know you just woke up, angel, but you still need more rest, I can see it." He looked at Whistler. "You both do. I've found it's best not to travel at night anyhow. We can leave at morning light. I'll keep watch over us until then." Whistler began to protest but John held up a calloused hand. "I'm gonna be honest. You two look like hell itself has run over you. I should know." He laughed. "You need a bit more peace and I'm the man to give it to ya."

Whistler felt his tiredness fully for the first time then. John's story had been so invigorating that it had temporarily distracted him, but he knew he was still worn, maybe always would be. A few more hours of sleep with John keeping watch might be just what he needed.

"Alright," Whistler said. "It was a boon to meet you, John."

"You help me get to the machine," John said, "and the scales'll be weighed in your favor."

△

John Henry had not only kept watch all night but had also managed to kill two rabbits and harvest some delicious red berries. The food hummed in Whistler's stomach, shot energy through his limbs.

He'd slept surprisingly well and now he stood up. His wounded leg felt a different type of awful. The blood that had soaked his pant leg was no longer flowing. The scab was purple and dirty, but he didn't see the red rim of infection. His arm seemed in similarly decent condition.

The angel's iridescent robe, which the day before had been dirty, wrinkled, and coated in all manner of blood, was as clean as when he had fallen to earth. His face was healed as well.

John had been right. That one night had done them a world of good.

The large black man was slinging his pack on his back and shouldering his hammers now, and Whistler knew it was time to move on. He gazed to the southwest and could still see the rift in the landscape that the tornado had left.

He heard John's hammer heads clink together and felt a moment of panic that a demon was attacking, but the black man simply seemed to be feeling the land as he had described in his account.

"Musta been a hell of a storm," he said. "How long ago?"

"Five years," Whistler answered.

"That long?" John whistled. "The earth ain't even sorted out yet. Life's havin' a hard time livin' under the path of that storm. Definitely somethin' special about it."

"It's as stark a path as I've ever seen," the angel agreed.

"Well then let's use these legs that God gave us," John said. "And these eyes, too. Keep 'em open."

Whistler took Black's reigns. The animal whinnied and Whistler patted his nose to calm him. "It's alright," he said. "We'll get back home someday." He turned and looked over his shoulder. "Maybe."

$$\triangle$$

The first three days of walking were still nerve-racking for Whistler. Things had been quiet and uneventful, but that didn't bring him much solace. The longer the silence lasted, the more Whistler's anticipation built. He began to see things. His mind was expecting something to happen, and nothing was, so it made up its own happenings to occupy itself. Even though the quiet times had unnerved Whistler's mind, they had given his arm and leg time to mend. He still had to be careful with them, of course, but they were starting to feel stronger.

Eventually, when the party lost the tornado's trail by sight, John had to feel their way forward with his Touch, clanking his hammers together and sensing the torn earth hidden beneath the grassy surface.

Early one morning John Henry stopped in his tracks. "I feel buildings," he said. "I feel railroad tracks, too."

"A town?" Whistler asked.

"Maybe," John said. "But there's somethin' wrong."

Whistler peered into the distance, trying to see any sign of what John spoke of, but he couldn't. "What do you mean something's wrong?" Whistler's left hand tightened on the handle of his scythe and his right tightened on Black's reigns.

"I don't feel any feet," John said.

"Ghost town, maybe," Whistler said. He looked at Black. The horse's ears were back. "Not somethin' we probably need to be going into right now."

"Maybe everyone is inside the buildings and you can't feel their feet against the earth," the angel suggested.

John walked a few steps forward and clanked his hammer heads in a complex rhythm. He concentrated, squinting in the silent, bright morning. His mouth opened slowly. His arms were shaking. "I can feel the machine," he said. "It's in there. Right in the center. I'm goin'. I don't feel any demons. If the machine's unguarded I'll . . . I'll just crush it."

"They could be baiting you, John Henry," the angel noted.

"Nah," John said.

"Yeah, John," Whistler replied. "I'd be wary of a trap."

"It's been ten years," John said. "Maybe they just moved on to doin' other things. Ruinin' other lives. Machine's probably been sittin' here collectin' rust. Well . . . I'll make sure it's never used again." He began to walk forward.

"He's not going to be easily stopped," the angel whispered to Whistler. "Look at the set of his jaw. Are we going to follow him?"

"I don't think we have a choice," Whistler hissed back. "He saved our lives, angel. We can't just abandon him now."

The angel unfurled his long fingers and glanced around warily and followed. Whistler did the same. Rooftops began to peek up over the horizon after a few minutes and Whistler got a sinking feeling in his stomach when he saw what lay ahead. The earth began to gray, the grasses becoming sickly and sparse. The closer they got to the town the worse the desolation got. John held a hammer in each hand. The caw of a lone crow sent a shiver up Whistler's spine. The bird was strutting back and forth on the roof of a dilapidated house.

John's boots crunched on gravel and then he stepped onto the railroad tracks, standing in between the rails looking for all the world as if he owned the whole town.

Whistler saw the machine now, about a hundred feet away resting in an overgrown patch of dead, brown weeds. There was no real reason for it to be here, he realized, as there was no rock to bore through. It had to be the bait that the angel suspected it was.

The machine was rusted. It teetered on the brink of falling over because one of its legs was twisted and broken.

John began to shake with laughter. "This whole time," he gasped. "This whole journey. All my healin'. All my work. All my sacrifice!" He took off running towards the machine.

"John, wait! No!" Whistler ran after John as fast as he could, but there was no way he could keep pace.

John was running so fast that he barely seemed in

control of his body. The heads of his hammers clinked furiously, making rapid complex rhythms. It was frantic music. John brought his hammers behind his back and then, just as he reached the machine, swung them both downward with such force that the earth heaved and exploded upward with a boom, knocking Whistler off of his feet and causing Black to dance away in fear. A gigantic fountain of dirt obscured Whistler's vision of John and the machine for a full minute. He stood still, his heart pounding, his mouth hanging open, praying that John hadn't killed himself in his moment of glory.

When the earth and dust settled, John stood next to the scattered remains of the machine, his head and shoulders piled with earth.

Whistler was tense, feeling that demons would stream from the haunted buildings and tear the three travelers to shreds. His skin prickled when he heard a noise from behind him. He wheeled around quickly.

A brown horse was galloping towards the abandoned town, dust flying in its wake. The man riding the horse was terrified, bent low over the animal.

On the run from demons, same as us? Whistler wondered.

But then, while Whistler's mind was still deciding what to do, he saw another horse burst through the dust cloud that the first one had kicked up. This horse was pure white and its rider's blond hair blew out behind her in the wind.

It's a woman, Whistler realized in amazement. For a moment his heart ached for his wife - he wondered for a split-second if it was her - and the pain he felt inside was sharp. It wasn't her. Would probably never be her.

This woman wore tall boots, a divided riding skirt, and Whistler could have sworn that medals adorned her tight-fitting brown tunic. She had something strapped to her back that glinted in the sun.

"What kind of humans are these?" the angel asked.

"I don't know," Whistler said. "But that woman is gonna get herself killed doin' that."

The man riding in front of the woman looked horrified, though. Then the woman pulled the glinting object from her back and held it up.

It's a rifle. There's no way she can make that shot. Gotta be at least seven-hundred paces or more.

Whistler saw the woman shoot before he heard it. The bullet was fiery orange, looking like a meteor streaking through the dust cloud. Then the sound reached him.

BLAM!

The male rider's arm sprayed blood.

Whistler found his mouth hanging open.

"It's . . . the Touch," John said. He'd come up behind Whistler and the angel, not having bothered to clean himself off. "Not my Touch. Some other kind."

The wounded rider careened into town, his terrified horse frothing. He didn't appear to notice Whistler, John, or the angel. He leaped from his horse, pulled a pistol from a belt holster, and dove into a building twenty feet from where Whistler stood.

The woman pulled up her horse and vaulted from its back.

"Get out of there!" she hollered up at the building. She waited with her rifle tucked to her shoulder and scanned the windows of the building. She was muttering to herself, cursing. "Don't think I'm gonna forgive you for what you done!"

Whistler tried to approach her. "I . . . uh, do you . . . uh . . . do you need-"

BLAM!

The fiery bullet streaked from the end of the woman's gun into the highest window of the house.

"-any help?" Whistler finished.

The woman - no, she was more of a girl as Whistler got a closer look at her - lowered her rifle and turned to face him. She couldn't have been more than thirteen years of age. Her face was stern, her eyes had the look of a hawk. She might have been crying, it was hard to tell. Her blond hair and clothing were dusty, but Whistler had been right; medals were pinned across her chest. Her rifle was in pristine condition, polished and obviously well taken care of.

"Damn," she said. She looked slowly over at Whistler, John, and the angel. "The hell you three doin' out here? A farmer, a slave, and some weirdo all standin' in a deserted town?" She raised her rifle and sighted along it. "Seems suspicious."

Whistler set his scythe on the ground and slowly held up his hands. "We mean you no harm," he said. "My name's Whistler. This here's John Henry. And this one . . . is an angel."

"You expect me to believe that after what I been though?"

"I don't know what you've been through."

"We can all be on our way," the girl said. "Don't take another step towards me. I can shoot the legs off a flea from a half-mile out." She started to back away.

Something stirred in Whistler's memory. He'd heard of a woman like this.

"Pardon me for askin'," Whistler said. "But you wouldn't happen to be Annie Oakley, would ya?"

The woman got a look on her face as if she'd just swallowed poison. She spit off to the side. "Naw," she said. "She's the one that got me into this mess. My name's Lillian

Smith. You remember it well, now."

After what Whistler had just seen he figured he'd probably never forget it.

△

"I don't know how I feel about havin' a murderer travelin' with us," Whistler said. The man Lillian had shot at had never emerged from the building, and he guessed that Lillian, through some kind of odd luck, had killed him, sight unseen, with that one shot.

Whistler, John, and the angel were still standing in the middle of the deserted town, and Lillian was a little ways off seeing to her horse, cooing over it; suddenly she was a completely different person from the maniac that Whistler had seen earlier.

"She's-" the angel began.

"I know," Whistler interrupted. "She's Fire. A Hero. I saw the bullets she fired as well as you two did."

"It's all falling into place so quickly," the angel whispered. "When I was Called here I was ready to stay for any length of time. An Eon, to an angel, isn't really that long. But we've gotten three of the pieces in less than the time of an Earth week."

"We haven't 'got' her yet, angel," Whistler said. "She just *murdered* that man. My hair's still standin' on end."

John shook his head. "It's not the killin' that's botherin' ya, Whistler. It's the not knowin' why. Besides, it might not have been a man at all."

"John's right," the angel said, touching his long fingertips together. "It could have been a lesser demon, like the ones that ran the digging machine."

"I'll go into that building and find out," John said, shouldering his hammers. "I'll know if it's a demon when I look at it."

"We should all go," Whistler said.

"No need," John said. "You stay safe out here. I've been around enough demons to know what I'm doin'." He turned and walked towards the building.

"Alright," the angel agreed. "Exercise caution, John. Whistler, we need to talk to Lillian. It would be beneficial to find out if she is on the same path as us. And to maybe give her an opportunity to justify her actions."

"You mustn't like it anymore than I do," Whistler said.

The angel shook his head. "Once I knew I was headed to Earth, I was prepared for anything. Morality plays a big part in this whole journey. You've never killed anyone. We heard John's story. He might have *meant* to kill folks but he never did. We have to let her tell her story, Whistler. We can't just outright ask her. I have a feeling we might . . . frighten her if we accuse her. She doesn't appear stable right now."

Whistler sighed. "She's a fine shot. It'd be nice to have her along."

The angel nodded his agreement.

"Well then," Whistler said, "who's doin' the talkin'?"

"Well, you-"

"I know. I'm the Hero."

Whistler walked up behind Lillian, making sure to make plenty of noise so she knew he was coming. She was brushing out her horse and talking to it. Her rifle hung diagonally across her back, various packs were strewn around her feet on the dusty ground.

Whistler cleared his throat.

"You still here?" Lillian asked without turning around.

"Yeah," Whistler said.

"Just seems strange. Three weird people hanging around in a deserted town. You part of some kind of smuggling ring?"

"No," Whistler said.

"Are ya bandits?"

"No."

"You here to arrest me?"

Whistler wondered if she was trying to rile him. He wasn't easily riled. "None of those things," he said. "Um . . . where are you headed?"

"Nosy, aren't ya?"

"Don't you see this tall fellow standing next to me?" Whistler asked. "He's an angel. An *angel*. Like from heaven. Out of the bible."

Lillian turned around. "Look, I don't care much for religion. And as far as this guy, I've seen weirder lookin' people."

"You've got powers," Whistler said. "So do I. We're the same. At the very least it behooves you to talk to us."

Lillian's eyes narrowed. "Think I'm stupid, do ya? I got no interest in tellin' you a lick about myself. I got no time to wait around. You prove to me right now that what you say is true, old farmer, because I'm ready to ride and I don't like to be kept. Prove to me you're magic and we can talk. Otherwise you're just another blatherin' dimwit in a world that's already full of 'em."

Whistler stared flatly at Lillian. Then he brought his lips together and blew a single high note. The sound tore through the air. Both Black and Lillian's horse took notice, immediately coming to where Whistler stood and facing him attentively.

Then the brown horse that the man had been riding galloped into town. All three mounts now stood in front of Whistler, ears pricked in interest.

"One for everybody if you ride with us," Whistler said calmly.

△

Lillian stood still, a look of awe on her face. "I . . . I'm sorry," she said carefully. "I'm just . . . confused lately. I guess it's a thing with me nowadays. Look, you don't know what I been through, but ya seem nice enough. Didn't mean to get us off to a rough start. Speak your peace. I'll hear you out, at least."

John's boots crunched over the ground and Whistler turned to look at him. John nodded at Whistler.

So the man in the building was *a demon.*

"Looks like we got some things to sort out now that yer listenin'," Whistler said to Lillian. "I'm gonna try to make this simple and quick." He put his hand on his chest. "I'm a farmer. A Venturer: a Hero of air. My farm was destroyed not too long ago and I'm following the path of a tornado that tore through this area five years ago in hopes that the wind will lead me to the place I'm supposed to go." It felt so short when he put it that way. "John Henry was a slave turned prisoner turned worker. He's a Forger: a Hero of earth. He fought his way across the country to get vengeance on the machine that helped take his friend's life. And this is the angel. He's a creature that I called here accidentally, and now we're all wrapped up in some kind of quest. A real life tall tale, if ya will. Maybe you're wrapped up in it now too, Lillian, but . . . we're gonna need ta know more about ya."

Lillian nodded and stayed silent for a while. "What is it that you think I am?" she finally asked the angel.

"At the very least you've got fire magic," he replied. "You can tell us more about that in a bit. The mere fact that you've crossed paths with us means you are likely much more than you even suspect. Fire Heroes are called Rebels. They're often hot-tempered and dislike the trappings of society. They'll try to settle in somewhere, but it won't last. Unlike Venturers they don't want to be free from places, but rather from people."

"Oh, ain't that the truth!"

The angel nodded.

We've got a hook in her, Whistler thought. *Now we just need to be gentle with her.* He saw a trace of fear behind Lillian's eyes. What the angel had said was probably right: if they spooked her, she would run, and they would lose her.

"Everyone's spillin' their stories rather easily around here," Lillian noted. "Is that what this is? A group of storytellers?"

"It's better than travelin' in silence," John said gently. "Besides, if this is a quest we gotta know who our partners are."

"Ya wanna know about me?" Lillian asked. "Not sure I got much left to lose, even if this turns out to be a mistake." She started packing her things. "Well, we can ride and talk unless you got need to rest. I got nowhere to be and I don't answer to anyone anymore." She glanced briefly at the building that held the dead demon, mouthed a few words, then swung herself up onto her white horse. "Lead on. I'll follow for a spell. You want me to start at the beginning?"

"It's usually a very good idea," the angel said.

"That was a joke."

"Oh."

△ CHAPTER 16 △

"I won't *have* it!" Lillian's mother shouted. "Bill Smith you are a wrathful son of a bitch!"

Lillian lay in her small room, pillows pressed up against the sides of her face, their cool surfaces becoming hot. She turned them quickly during a moment of silence to get to the cool sides again.

There was a crash in the kitchen. Lillian heard her father's low voice, gruff and quiet. He never raised it.

"We got one of each, Bill," Lillian's mother shouted. "Do what you want with Joseph, but leave my Lillian alone. You tryin' ta make her into somethin' unnatural! You ain't right with the Lord, Bill. You ain't right with Him!"

Her father said something else, but it was lost beneath the stomping of feet.

"I told you not to encourage this anymore, but you won't listen to me, Bill! I have half a mind to-"

Lillian pressed the pillows harder against her ears, her heart pounding as her mother raged. She was a good woman, but her temper could get the best of her and Lillian's father was usually the target.

Why couldn't her father explain things to her mother? Couldn't the woman see that Lillian wasn't fit to sew and cook; had never had the slightest inclination or talent to do either of those things? She'd had scrapes on her knees and knots in her hair for almost all eight years of her life, much to her mother's chagrin.

Things were coming to a boil again now. She heard muffled yelling and quick footsteps, banging of dishes. Now Joseph, Lillian's brother, was yelling. He shouldn't be getting involved; things were bad enough already.

Lillian's hands started itching. She moved her palms

slowly against the pillows to try and stop it, but she knew that once it started it would only stop when she used her rifle again. That was the way it was for her. Her emotions were high, her body was primed to shoot.

Lillian glanced over at her rifle. The weapon leaned in the corner, the sunlight bouncing off the stock's metal inlay. Lillian had only gotten the rifle a few weeks ago and she already knew every inch of it. She knew how it was weighted, knew what it felt like, knew how fast and far it could fire, knew that she had to aim a hair's width to the left of whatever she wanted to hit. It was a serious upgrade from her old rifle. Her father must have spent a small fortune on it.

Her door opened the slightest crack, startling her, and she shut her eyes and tried to pretend to be asleep. There was a shuffling sound in the far corner of her room and then her father's footsteps retreated slowly back out the door.

She knew what would be missing when she opened her eyes.

$$\triangle$$

Lillian stared at the lump of dough in front of her. It was a sticky, wet mess and one of her hairs was already twined through it. Flour was piled all around it, but Lillian couldn't remember what the next step was or what she supposed to be doing. She stuffed her hands into the dough, the coolness of it temporarily banishing the itching in her palms.

"Lillian!" her mother snapped.

The girl tried to draw her hands out of the dough, but it stuck to them and ended up almost falling off of the table and onto the floor. That probably would have been a catastrophe. As it was, it was only a disaster.

"You're being purposely dense, Lillian! This is not difficult if you set your mind to it."

Lillian coerced her dough off of her hands and back onto the wooden table. She felt tears starting to form in her eyes as she looked over at her mother's perfectly round ball of dough. It glowed warmly in the daylight that streamed through the window. Then she looked back at her own.

She imagined a target on it. She knew that she could shoot this wad of dough from a hundred paces and hit it dead center.

Her parents had had arguments about her before, but her father had always come to her afterwards, a gleam in his eye. He always had mischief dancing about him. But not this time. Lillian's rifle had been taken and she couldn't find it anywhere. She feared it was gone for good.

"Look, Lillian, I know . . . what you must be thinking. But I'm not trying to punish you. It's just not proper for a little girl to be shooting guns at all hours. At any hour! People in the town already talk and I . . ." Her mother sighed and began kneading her dough. "All I ever wanted was a little . . . girl who I . . . I don't know." Lillian realized her mother was crying, but that only made things more confusing for her, and she took in none of the important things that the woman was trying to say. "My sister died so young that I never got the chance . . ." Her mother sighed. "Well. I just what what's best for you."

It was the last time her mother ever talked to her like that. Lillian would think back on that day and curse herself that she hadn't responded, hadn't been mature enough to say something meaningful.

As it was, since she was only eight, Lillian's mind had drifted back to more comfortable lines of thought.

Maybe my father is just taking longer than normal,

trying to lull mother into a false sense of security, then he'll take me and Joseph out shooting again.

BLAM!

Lillian heard the gunshot come from the north. The target range. Her heart dropped. *They're out without me!* She bolted up from the table, ran to her room and buried herself in her pillows, getting dough all over her bed in the process.

△ CHAPTER 17 △

The town was always bustling on Sundays and Lillian found herself on a busy street picking at the knot that held her bonnet firmly to her head. Her mother, father, and brother were somewhere on these gravel streets, but Lillian had lost sight of them. She'd never been to this part of the town before.

She wasn't nervous, though: her family wouldn't leave without her, and on the way in she had spied a store with some very interesting guns in the window. She couldn't remember exactly which window the guns had been in, so she was backtracking, hoping to find the store before her family found her. She just wanted a glimpse at the weapons.

What she found was actually better.

Lillian had always been stubborn about a lot of things that her mother wanted her to do, but reading had never been one of them. She'd always been enamored of the beautiful, swirling letters that adorned the stocks and barrels of the rifles she'd fired. She had wanted to know how to read so she could better understand the weapons. Now her ability to read came in handy.

A wooden sign painted in bright red letters proclaimed:

MARKSMANSHIP CONTEST
TARGETS, CANS, BIRDS, MOUNTED, COINS
TEN O CLOCK, OCTOBER 19th
REGISTER WITHIN – LIMITED ENTRANCE

Someone bumped into her shoulder. Lillian stopped staring at the sign and looked over to see Harold Highwater, a boy about her age. He had sandy hair and was dressed well. But he was ugly. Something about him always made Lillian think of curdled milk.

"Lillian!" Harold said.

"Whaddya want?" She was suspicious.

"Word 'round here is that you're the best shooter in town. I had no idea." He bowed low.

Lillian's eyes narrowed. She recognized the mocking tone in the boy's voice. The thing her mother had said came back to her. They *were* talking about her in the town. She tried to push past Harold but he blocked her way. "Leave me alone," she said.

"Think you can shoot better than me?" he asked. "I never seen a girl with a rifle before. Bet it's real cute. Like a little deadly lady. You gonna sign up for the shootin' kawntest?" He said it dumbly, making fun of her.

Lillian felt her face grow red. Here she was, stuffed into clothes she hated, suffering sarcasm from a moron.

"I'm just out with my family," Lillian said.

"Oh," Harold said, wearing a mock-innocent look on his face while he glanced around. "Where are they?"

"It's none of your business."

"I think you should go for it," the boy said, indicating the contest sign. "If you enter and don't manage to shoot yourself in your own foot, why, I'll let you kiss me!"

"You're disgusting," Lillian said. She took a step backward. "Get away from me."

"Aw shucks. I might just let you kiss me anyway!" Harold leaned his face in close and Lillian's fist flew at it with amazing speed. Shooting wasn't the only thing she'd learned from her father and brother.

The boy backpedaled and screamed, blood leaking from his nose. "Ack!" he yelled. "You're like a man! No one'll ever wanna marry you!" He screamed a string of curses.

"What's happening over here?" Harold's father was pointing at Lillian and shouting, but she was already running. She'd learned much in that brief encounter. She learned that she hated boys and she also learned that nothing would be better than besting them at every skill they held dear.

Come hell or high water she would *be* in that contest.

△

But they wouldn't let her in.

Actually, word had gotten around about Lillian's short-lived fight with Harold and she wasn't even allowed out of the house until the following Sunday. When she had finally sneaked her way back to the store (knowing full well there would be consequences) the owner wouldn't let her enter the contest, making it clear that it was for men only. She had thought the real problem would have been that she was only eight years old, but it had been that she was a girl. The old store owner had almost looked apologetic as he had denied her request, but Lillian couldn't be sure that he wasn't just mocking her. Or perhaps he thought her slow and was being extra nice, as if she should have been smart enough to know that what she was trying to do was ridiculous.

At home, she continued to hear gunshots coming from north of her house and each time she heard one it pierced her soul. Her hands longed to hold a rifle, to fire at something, to do what she wanted to do. But, as her mother kept telling her, 'people can't do what they want all the time.'

Lillian began to add 'if they follow the rules' in her head whenever her mother said that.

△

By now, no matter how much Lillian wanted it, she knew that she wouldn't be allowed to enter the shooting contest. She had put together all sorts of plans but they all fell apart in her head. They all went something like this: dress as boy, sneak away from family, obtain rifle, come up with contest entrance fee, convince store owner . . . The list was too long. It just wasn't going to happen. She was stubborn, but she knew impossible when she saw it.

She had to set her sights on something smaller. Just being able to *watch* the contest, to catch even a glimpse of it, might be enough. Lillian remembered Joseph getting in trouble at the dinner table once for talking about how old Mr. James couldn't be without a bottle. Lillian hadn't known what that meant, but now she imagined she probably felt like Mr. James: unable to be apart from guns without feeling empty. *Poor Mr. James!* she thought. *Just let him have his bottle!*

Her family was in town on the day of the contest. They hadn't known it, and hadn't come specifically for it, but Lillian was now sweating and shaking in church, waiting for her opportunity to escape.

"Is there something wrong with you?" Joseph whispered to her during the sermon.

"I just don't feel well," Lillian responded meekly.

Lillian's mother shot them both a look.

"She's gonna be sick, mom," Joseph whispered.

"Be quiet the both of you," her mother hissed.

What Lillian's brother had said probably wasn't far from the truth. Lillian was a bundle of nerves and her stomach was flipping. Her family usually went out to the town after church. That was where she had lost them before, and that's where she planned to lose them again. This time it was going to be harder, though. She had to stay gone for at least three hours. Surely they would come looking for her. So she sat in church, kicking her legs and trying not to feel sick with worry.

The sermon lasted an interminably long time, but finally church was over and Lillian followed her family down the aisle, slow and mopey, knowing she was coming close to her opportunity, and feeling deep down that she would fail. She began to feel sad, nervous, and anxious all at the same time, and her hands itched so terribly that she wanted to tear the skin off.

She almost got out of the church before she threw up.

Lillian heard her mother apologizing to the preacher, and then her father said: "Take her to the wagon, Joseph. Make sure she lays down."

Lillian's mind began to work the instant these new wheels were set into motion. She looked up into her brother's eyes as he took her hand and knew her chance had come.

$$\triangle$$

"You look like you're up to something," Joseph said as he escorted Lillian back to the wagon.

He's fifteen. He's smart. He knows.

Her silence was evidence enough.

"Look, you'd better just tell me," he said. "This has to do with the shooting contest, doesn't it?"

Lillian felt her eyes grow to twice their size.

"Yeah, I know," Joseph continued. "I'm the one that

had to apologize to Harold's dad because you punched his son in the nose. I saw the sign for the contest as well as you did. I know you, Lil."

Lillian remained quiet, choosing to simply stare at the soft grass under her feet.

"I stuck up for you the night mom and dad took your rifle away. Almost got me kicked out of the house, but I did it. I think you're good, and I think it's a shame what our parents are doing."

"I'm not gonna shoot in it," Lillian said meekly. "But I've gotta see it, Joseph. I. Have. To."

Joseph gave her an appraising look. "You got quite the spirit for one so young. And a girl, too. There's no one else in this town quite like you. You're gonna catch hell for this. You know that."

"Yeah."

"And you're willing to do it anyway?"

"Yeah."

"Lil," Joseph said, setting his big hand on her small shoulder, "that's either really brave or really stupid, and probably a mix of both."

△

"I love you, Lil," Joseph said. "But you're still gonna owe me somethin' big for this." He was busy helping her arrange blankets into a Lillian-shaped bundle that lay in the wagon bed, but there would be no Lillian inside.

"Anything," Lillian said, her heart pounding.

"I tucked you into the wagon and then I went back and I know nothing else. I didn't help you, I wasn't a part of this. I'll dissuade them from checking on you when we leave for home, but I can't promise anything." He stood up and brushed his hands together. "Looks good," he said, nodding approvingly at their deception. "Now get the hell outta here and find a good place to hide."

Lillian turned to go, her feet flying.

△

Lillian could see the contest site. A crowd of people surrounded men on horseback. The men sat tall, all manner of beautiful weapons attached to their hips and backs. Lillian thought she saw one of the men sighting down a rifle just like the one her father had bought her and she got so excited that she almost fell off the roof.

She had clambered up the side of the general store and was sitting with her back to a rather conveniently placed window buttress. The sun was high in the sky, but it left just enough shadow for Lillian to melt into.

Her eyes had always been sharp and even from this distance she could see every detail. Colorful cans were lined up on fences with many more cans in reserve, stacked on the ground nearby. Targets of all shapes and sizes hung from posts, and Lillian even saw a few live birds being kept in cages. She supposed they would be released, get a fair chance at flight, and then be shot down.

It was then that she realized the scope of the contest. She hadn't been thinking. This thing was huge. It had to be the event of the year. That was when she realized that her family had purposely not talked about this. This was something her brother and father would have loved, but they weren't going to go to it because of Lillian.

It was why Joseph had told her to hide once she'd gotten here. Lillian's plan had involved standing right in the midst of this crowd, but she now saw the wisdom in her brother's words. People in the town were talking about her. They would have known she wasn't supposed to be here.

The whole place was against her and Joseph knew it.

It took her eight-year-old brain a few moments to start to realize something that wouldn't sink in fully until years later: her mother now had complete control of the family, and much more sway in the town than Lillian had ever realized. Lillian was suddenly terrified, but the contest was starting and all other thoughts were muted.

It was unlike anything she'd ever seen.

There were twenty contestants in all. Each had been introduced to the crowd, their names lost on the wind, but Lillian could see their faces. Her heart felt like it was up in her throat as she gazed on them. To her, they were all heroes, men of legend. It didn't matter that she'd seen her father and her brother shoot, didn't matter that she was a shooter herself. She only recognized three of the men from her town, the rest were from elsewhere.

Heroes from Elsewhere.

The contest started with target shooting. Simple. Straightforward. Here is a thing, now shoot it as dead center as you can. None of the men failed to hit the target, but two of the men's bullets punched noticeably farther out from the center than the rest. Lillian could have told both men what they'd done wrong.

It was time to shoot the cans, and bullets blew the metal things off of their perches with the force of lightning strikes. At this distance, the satisfying pings of bullets hitting metal came later than the image of the cans flying into the air. Where target shooting had been just one at a time, this was a race to shoot all the cans off. It meant aiming and shooting all in rapid succession, bullet casings dropping to the ground, in a lovely cascade.

The crowd cheered as the men who had done well raised their hands in the air.

Now five of the men walked off to the sides. Lillian

wasn't sure of the rules, but it seemed that they were done.
Two of them were the ones who had been furthest off center
on the target shooting, and the other three had been sluggish
in their attempts to fell the cans.

The crowd shifted and the remaining men
remounted their horses and lined up to take their chances at
the next challenge. The target was tilted and they would be
firing at an odd angle, riding perpendicular to it. Three of
them outright failed to hit it as their horses sped past. They
were done.

The birds were released and some fell and some
escaped. There must have been a trick to this because Lillian
watched men with easy shots wait and wait. She surmised
that the farther away from the shooter the bird was felled
the better. Some men gambled too hard and lost, letting the
birds get too far away, making their shots impossible.
Lillian knew the instant it happened and she cringed,
knowing that the men who missed wouldn't make it to the
next round.

There were fewer and fewer heroes.

Nothing lasted long enough for Lillian's taste. She
could have watched each event for an eternity. It whizzed
by too quickly, the rest of the world forgotten. It didn't even
cross her mind that her parents were probably home by now,
had discovered her absence, and were likely on their way
back. It didn't matter.

She thought of what the sign had said.

Coins.

It seemed insane. Coins were tiny, not much wider
than bullets themselves. Maybe they could be hung by a
string and shot at, but the shooter would have to be
fantastically close and also pray there was very little wind.
Not for their bullet - even Lillian knew how to compensate
for the wind - but so that the coin didn't swivel around and

be, at times, thin as a blade of grass as it spun. They'd have
to-

No. A man stood with his hand outstretched,
something resting on top of his second finger, his thumb
under it.

He's going to flip *it?*

Lillian sat bolt upright in her shadow on the roof,
her heart pounding. This was something she didn't want to
miss. She willed her eyes to focus more sharply, knowing
the request was likely to fail, but she felt something happen
behind them anyway. The muscles complained, but
suddenly things became crystal. She'd never seen the world
in this much detail before; the clarity was astounding. At
this distance she shouldn't have been able to make out the
detailed images on the coin, but she could.

The first man stepped up, shouldered his rifle. The
coin was flipped and the man's shot missed it. The bullet
went wide. Lillian wasn't surprised. She found herself
considering it impossible to hit a coin from that far away.
She'd never even fantasized about such a ridiculous thing.

The second man patted the first on the shoulder and
stepped up to the line. He shouldered his rifle and readied
himself for failure.

Lillian watched the coin flip in the air. The man
who'd flipped it drew his arm back swiftly, and then Lillian
watched as the shooter fired. The bullet connected with the
coin, the moment of impact etched itself into Lillian's mind.
The man picked the coin up off the ground and held it
aloft, showing the crowd the clean hole through the center
of it. The crowd erupted.

Lillian had always considered herself to be good, but
she suddenly felt like nothing. She couldn't compare to the
man who had shot that rifle. She told herself it could have
been a lucky shot, but she knew deep down that it hadn't

been. She had seen the precision in the man's movements, had watched him adjust the shot using his breath, had seen how relaxed he had been when he'd pulled the trigger, and had marveled at the way he had almost *willed* the bullet to travel on the right path.

She had to meet him. Touch him. Something. Her hands would stop itching if she just went down there. She climbed off the roof and ran.

Lillian's heart beat frantically in her chest as she approached the shooting ground. The crowd was still clapping, milling about, yelling praise, shouting at each other, paying wagers. Lillian slipped through unnoticed, her cheeks burning, flushed with blood.

She let a mixture of youthful bravery and stupidity guide her towards her target. The man who'd won the contest was standing with his back to her. He was talking to a few other men and slowly taking off his gloves. Lillian was short, only coming up to his belt. Suddenly she felt a midget in a world of giants. Panic started to set in, but Lillian reached out and tapped the man on the back.

"Excuse me a moment, gentlemen," he said to the men he was talking to.

When he turned around Lillian's breath caught in her throat. He had deep blue eyes that pierced hers. He looked as if he were about to tell her that he was busy, but an interested look flashed over his face for a moment.

"Hi," he said, kneeling down. "What's your name, sweetheart?"

He thinks I'm some kind of stupid girl! Oh, God, I am a stupid girl! Say you're a shooter, Lillian. Say you're like him. Say you've never seen anything so amazing. Say it! Say it!

But she had forgotten what her name was. She thought really hard. "Lillian," she said finally. She was almost sure that was right.

"I'm Frank," the man said. "Frank Butler. You live around here?"

"Yes," Lillian stammered. "Down the road a ways. I'm Lillian."

"I know," Frank chuckled. "You've said as much."

He was studying her, Lillian decided. She'd only wanted to say hi, but now she found herself under his gaze. She began to sweat even more. He couldn't have been more than a few years older than Joseph, but he looked so wise, so beautiful. And he was staring into her eyes.

The world slowed around Lillian, conversations were muted, and she felt her hands grow hot. Frank reached out and took one of them. His huge hand eclipsed Lillian's small one.

"Your eyes," he said. "Your hands. How old are you?"

"Eight."

"Never seen one so young before."

"What . . . what do you mean?" Lillian stammered again.

"You can shoot," Frank said.

Yes! Yes I can! He knows! How does he know?

Lillian stood mute, staring into Frank's face.

"Frank, get over here!" a man yelled. "Gotta get a photograph of the winner!"

"I'll come back for you," Frank said to Lillian. "I'll come back." Then he disappeared into the crowd and Lillian ran.

△ CHAPTER 18 △

Lillian shouldered her rifle and pulled the trigger, then she switched the rifle to her other shoulder and shot again. The pine cones that hung from the tree exploded at each of her shots, showering their seeds towards the ground. Lillian pumped the action once and then, forcing her eyes to focus, took aim at one of the tiny seeds.

Her vision became crystal and she watched her shot obliterate the seed.

"That shot was for you, Frank," she muttered.

She'd been waiting five years for Frank to come back for her. Her days were spent shooting when she could sneak away, and her nights were spent in torture. She dreamed of Frank, of his handsome face and deep eyes. Lillian didn't know what other thirteen-year-old girls wanted. She didn't care.

Only a few more years and I can marry him, she thought for the millionth time.

Her mother had always been preparing her for marriage anyway, maybe she would approve of the union. *Oh, wouldn't it be amazing?!* Lillian trudged back through the snow to her house. Her self-imposed bullet quota for the day had run out and she was tired.

She threw off her snow gear, hid her rifle in her room, and trudged over to the table, content for now to be alone on this quiet Sunday. She'd had to pitch an enormous fit to get out of going to town with her family. In the end her parents had gotten fed up with her. Well, they couldn't drag her anymore; she was a big girl, she could choose some things for herself.

It was a testament to her strength.

Or is it a testament to the weakness of my family?

Lillian suddenly felt cold, even though the winter sun was burning warmly through the window. Her newfound freedom, the strength she felt; maybe it wasn't inner strength but outer weakness. Maybe she wasn't getting better, maybe everyone else was getting worse.

Her skin prickled as emotion welled within her. She always felt a terrifying fire burning inside of her these days. Shame and guilt suddenly collided inside. Her mother and father were always fighting over her, always working hard to compromise on what was best for her, and here she was defying everyone. They should have beaten her. Dragged her out to the wagon. Forced her to go to town today. *I'm a child. What am I thinking?* Suddenly the whole situation seemed wrong.

They've . . . they've given up on me. I'm . . . a burden.

Lillian heard the horses before she saw them. She heard their breathing, heavy in the winter air. She wiped the tears from her eyes and ran to the front window. Whoever it was, they were already here; the horse's hoof prints led around the side of the house. *It could be the Millers from next door.* Winter was a time of helping everyone out. Seemed there was always misfortune this time of year.

But Lillian knew who it really was. Could almost feel him through the walls.

When she opened the door, Frank Butler stood there, sunlight spilling in all around him. His eyes were as blue as Lillian remembered, his hair as black. He looked down at her and smiled, then glanced past her into the house.

"Hello, Miss Smith," he said. "Are your folks about?"

"You came back for me," Lillian whispered.

Frank laughed. His teeth were shiny and perfect. But now he was giving her a sad look. She knew how she must look to him: a desperate child, swooning like an idiot.

"Oh, I see," Frank said. "Yes. Um. Well, Lillian, I can wait for your folks if you'll let me stay. Are they in town?"

"They don't need to know," Lillian shot back. Her heart was racing, her mouth was dry. "Oh my God you're here. They don't need to know anything you tell me. Nothing. I've been waiting, Mr. Butler. Frank. Mr. Butler. I'm a good shot. A great shot. Let's go. When do we leave? Where are we going?" She watched a few snowflakes fall silently onto Frank's head and when he hesitated to respond to her outburst she remembered her manners and forced herself to calm down. "I expect my folks back any minute. Please, come in."

Lillian was overly conscious of herself now. As she led Frank into the house she tried to walk with dignity and poise. She tried sticking out her chest, swaying her hips. She wasn't sure if either thing worked. She was awkward, silent when she should have been making conversation. She began to blush, tried to stop. That only made her more flustered. By the time Lillian had led Frank to her father's chair her throat was tight and her hands were balled.

An eternity ticked by as the two sat in silence. Finally, just as Lillian was certain she would die, Frank began to talk.

"Guess there's no harm in telling you," he said. "First, let me say that I'm sorry it's been so long. Me bargin' in here after all these years seems kind of strange, I'm sure. But, Lillian, you're a Sharpshooter. Even beyond the normal definition of that word. I can see it in your eyes - the irises to be particular. Have you ever seen yourself in a really good mirror?"

Lillian shook her head. Her parents had a cracked, cloudy one that was about the size of her palm. She didn't suppose that counted.

"Well, your irises are ringed," Frank continued. "It's been explained to me that the eyes of a Sharpshooter work differently than those of normal men and women. One in three million. Those are the odds of being born as you are, so they say. Staggering, I know. But it's more than the eyes. There's a Fire inside of you that longs to burst free. Rebellion, anger, frustration. You can use these things when you shoot. Channel your feelings through your weapon." He laughed. "Oh, God, I haven't had to explain it in so long. It sounds kind of strange when I say it out loud." He leaned forward. "Do your hands burn?"

"All the time," Lillian said. "They itch and burn unless I'm shooting."

I'm something special! Maybe I could run away with him! We'll go off together. He can work with me. I'm going to escape all of the plans my mother has for me. No marriage to anyone. Anyone but Frank Butler, at least.

There was a knock at the door and Lillian jumped. Frank turned.

"That's probably her," he said. He stood and adjusted his hat and gloves. "I beat her here by a good fifteen minutes. That'll probably rankle her."

"Her who?" Lillian asked.

Frank opened the door and a beautiful woman with long, flowering hair strode through and into Frank's arms. They kissed and Lillian's entire body burned.

"This her?" the woman asked. "Oh, you were right, Frank. I can see it, even from here."

Frank escorted the woman over. Lillian was numb.

"Lillian I'd like you to meet your teacher. She'll help develop your skills as a Sharpshooter. This is my wife, Annie Oakley."

△

"Oh, I see," Whistler said.

"Yeah, I'll bet you do," Lillian spat back.

The small party was sitting around the fire on a particularly cold night. Lillian had easily shot a few rabbits for supper and John Henry turned them over a spit now. "He didn't mean nothin' by it, Lillian," the large man said.

Lillian stood up angrily. "This ain't just a story of unrequited love. Nothin' that childish. Nothin' that simple."

"Stories of this kind never are," the angel assured her. "Please, continue."

"Nah, I'm done talkin' for now," Lillian said. "I gotta think things over." She looked over the three of them. "The first man to lay a hand on me loses it."

Whistler thought he saw a tear slide down Lillian's cheek as she pulled her sleeping roll tightly around herself and her rifle. He watched the angel and John Henry sit in silence, simply listening to the rabbits crackle over the flame, until he too fell asleep.

△

"There was somethin' off about Buffalo Bill's Wild West," Lillian said, "that I couldn't put my finger on when I first got there."

Whistler, awakened by the morning conversation, rubbed his eyes and checked his injuries. They still pulled painfully, and his body still ached, but they were always getting better. The memory of the demon at his farm had haunted his dreams last night. He had imagined himself falling into its gaping mouth, serrated teeth ripping him to shreds. Between John Henry, the angel, and his new fiery companion, Whistler felt a bit safer, but he wondered if it was enough security to overcome what might lie ahead. He envisioned a stampede: the collected armies of Hell rising over the horizon, screaming in unison, longing to destroy him.

"What is this Buffalo Bill's Wild West?" the angel asked. He saw that Whistler was awake. "Have you heard of it, Whistler?"

Whistler nodded and sauntered over as best he could. "I've heard of it. One of the most famous spectacles the world has yet known, if I'm accurate on that."

Lillian scoffed. "More like a breeding ground for freaks and demons," she said. "What do ya think I killed back there?"

"So you *did* know the man you killed was a demon," Whistler said.

"Course I knew," Lillian said. "But I didn't wanna know." Her face changed and she turned to the angel. "Is that what this is about? You wanna know my story so you can judge me, angel?"

"It's part of it, certainly."

"Well, it's a relief i'n't?" John Henry asked. He slung his pack on his back and shouldered his hammers. "And, Lillian, ya can't be surprised that the angel cares 'bout stuff like that." He laughed. "He's from Heaven, after all! The White Palace!" John Henry clapped the tall creature on the shoulder.

"Something like that," the angel said, smiling.

"Well ya coulda just asked me," Lillian said. "I may be deadly, but I'm no killer."

"We didn't mean to offend, Lillian," Whistler said. "The angel wanted to hear it for himself. And we didn't wanna scare you off."

"You can tell much about a person from the stories

they tell," the angel agreed. "Short lies are much easier than long ones."

"So yer gonna be interested in the Wild West, then," Lillian said. "If ever there was a place to cleanse, that'd be it, angel. I'd take ya there, but I'm not sure where they've moved on to, and you'd have ta take me kickin' and screamin'." Lillian slung her rifle over her shoulder. "My story's still got a bit of details to it, though, so if we're still walkin' let's walk."

John bent to the ground and put his hand on it. "We're still on the right course," he said. "The path of the tornado is mighty wide."

Whistler squinted off into the distance. Anticipation rose within him, for he knew that if what the angel had said was true, there would only be one more person to collect. "On we go," he said, nodding. He Whistled for the horses and they came just as they had before. "Keep talkin', Lillian, and we'll keep listenin'."

△ CHAPTER 19 △

Buffalo Bill's Wild West had overwhelmed Lillian from the moment she had arrived.

It wasn't only because she'd left her family behind. It wasn't just because her father's proud look and her mother's disdainful one were burned into her memory, twin pride and shame. It wasn't even primarily because her emotions had been scattered to the winds by Frank Butler's cursedly perfect wife. No, it was mostly the sights, smells, and sounds of the place.

Lillian had ridden into the fair grounds on a dappled horse in between Frank Butler and Annie Oakley. She had been greeted by striped tents and raucous conversations: men and women yelling at Frank, whistling at Annie, asking questions about Lillian that all overlapped in a frenzy.

It had smelled like animals and odd spices that Lillian couldn't place. Her nose hadn't known what to make of any of it.

The colors had been so bright that at first they hurt her eyes, the pungent odors had hurt them as well, she had winced at the loud sounds: gunfire, animals trumpeting, shouts.

When Frank and Annie had stopped their horses that first time, Lillian had closed her eyes and slid down out of her saddle. Her boots had clicked on the dirt, hard-packed already from so many hooves, paws, and feet. The show had only been in North Platte for a few weeks and it had transformed the section of ground so that it looked as if it had always been there.

The show had become Lillian's home for the time being. She worked among the other performers, never quite fitting in, never quite being accepted, always feeling like an outsider. And always yearning after Frank.

Lillian would catch a glimpse of him at the show grounds only to have her romantic fantasy dashed as Frank grabbed hold of Annie's waist, or kissed her, or nodded his approval at her after a fine performance.

Annie acted the role of Lillian's tutor, teaching her things she had never known how to do before. Lillian learned how to Breathe, how to See, how to Aim, how to Trace. The skills were revealed to her by Annie's steady guidance while the Wild West surged and moved around her, going from city to city, tugging her along; not yet a full-fledged performer, but well on the way.

$$\triangle$$

Lillian was sitting on a wooden crate, watching the show be torn down bit by bit. It was time to move again as they so often did. The horses and wagons necessary to move the gigantic production to a new locale seemed a never-ending caravan. Lillian had done her part of the move already. She had to clean and pack her rifle, a few targets, some of the props for the trick-shot show, and her clothing and other necessities. In truth, she never felt as if she pulled enough of her weight, but she took her orders directly from Annie - or Frank if Annie wasn't around – and Annie never gave her any additional instructions during moves. The show thrived on routine.

Lillian felt so young sitting on the sidelines while the other performers shouted back and forth to each other as they ebulliently tore down the show. She swung her legs back and forth while she watched Frank load barrels onto a cart.

"Not bad to look at is he?"

Lillian started. She turned her head to see the last person she expected sitting next to her. Buffalo Bill was dressed in pale leather chaps and a coat with tassels. He was a strikingly trim man, all legs and power. He wore a three-corner hat that covered his forehead almost to his eyes, which were shrouded in shadow by the noon sun.

Lillian had had very little contact with Buffalo Bill since coming to the show. The thing was so wide and so large that certainly the man didn't have time to deal with a meager apprentice sharpshooter. Lillian had, of course, seen the man around the show – *his* show – but he'd never talked to her.

Lillian felt herself blushing. She bent her head so she was staring at the ground.

"Got a wild heart, that one does," Buffalo Bill said, indicating Frank. "I'd stay away from him."

"Yes, sir." There was something about Buffalo Bill that overwhelmed Lillian's senses. His presence was laced with ferocity and sureness all tucked inside of a calm man.

Buffalo Bill chuckled a bit. "A rifle shooter. I always wanted one around here. Annie insists on using a shotgun. If she weren't so damn good with it I'd have stopped her long ago." Buffalo Bill tossed something long and thin at Lillian.

The gun had come from nowhere, but Lillian grabbed it out of the air in sure hands.

"I have been watching you, Miss Smith. Your progress has been admirable. I've never seen one so young as you come so far, and I'll be damned if I wouldn't trust you with my life out on the range. Her name's Lucretia Borgia."

"Whose name, sir?"

"The gun's."

Lillian turned the weapon carefully in her hands. It

was a beautiful specimen, worn in all the right places.

"I don't need it anymore," Bill continued. "It's an upgrade to your current armament, and besides, I want you to have it."

"Why, sir?"

"Call it a hunch, Miss Smith. I feel there are hard, dark days ahead of us. Call it superstition. Had a dream last night that I was supposed to give this to you. Call it sentiment. I've got no kids of my own, but if I had one, I'd want her to shoot like you."

"Thank you, sir."

"We'll be teaming you up with Annie and trying out the new act in Iowa City. I'll leave it to you two and Frank to work out the choreography together. If all goes well, it'll be permanent."

Lillian's heart was beating so fast that she feared it would jump from her chest and run away.

"Bill!" someone shouted. "Quit makin' moves on the youngsters and get over here!"

Bill sprang off the crate, turned to Lillian, tipped his hat, and pointed at the rifle. "Treat her well," he said.

$$\triangle$$

"He *gave* you Lucretia Borgia?" Annie asked.

"I guess so." Lillian held her new weapon in one hand and her old one in the other.

"What does he think is going to happen? Bastard is accelerating things."

"What do you mean? I don't even think it's better than my old rifle . . ." Lillian began.

"It's a Focus, Lillian. Bill thinks you need to be better than you are right now. He's forcing my damn hand and I hate it when he does that. We need to redouble our efforts."

Lillian was taken aback. She'd never heard anything but praise from Annie in the year they had been working together. "I've been working as hard as I can," she said.

Annie sighed, her sharp eyes glittered. "Somethin's holdin' you back." She tapped Lillian's chest. "Somethin' in here. Now that you got Lucretia Borgia, well . . . I never thought Bill would part with that thing. Now I gotta tell you that you ain't been doin' as good as I thought you would." Annie was agitated, pacing now when Lillian had never known her to do that.

Lillian's chest became flush under her shirt. "I'm doin' everything you've been sayin'."

"Then it must be me. I'm not sayin' the right things. Look, Lillian, you got the physical skills. Eyes like a hawk. Arms steadier than a railway bridge. But somethin's missin'."

"Why are you tellin' me this now. Just cuz of this gun?"

"Because you're not giving your all," Annie said. "You're holding back. And there's been talk of . . . stopping your training."

Lillian panicked. "What? Why? Who's been talkin' about that? I'm as good as anyone here except you and Frank! I don't eat much! I behave! I do as I'm told! Maybe I need a new teacher! Maybe you're the problem!"

"Dammit, girl, this isn't a game," Annie hissed. "Oh, God." Annie leaned her shotgun against her leg, closed her eyes and rubbed her temples. "I shouldn't have listened to Frank. Shouldn't have brought you here. I haven't been fair with you, haven't told you what's really happening."

Annie motioned Lillian in through a heavy tent flap and closed it securely behind them. The inside of the tent was dark and heavy.

Annie turned around and looked Lillian in the eyes, held her gaze. "It's war, Lillian."

Lillian shivered. "What do you mean . . . war?"

"The Wild West is a front. All of it. The tents, the horses, the crowds, the actors, the talent. It's a mask for a greater operation. This isn't a circus, it's a training ground."

Lillian took a step backwards. The walls of the tent suddenly seemed to close in around her.

"Most shows like this are, truth be told," Annie continued. "The reason no one approaches you, the reason you feel alone is because I don't let anyone near you. You understand? Look, I'm taking a risk by trusting you here in this tent right now. Bill's played his hand by giving you that Focus rifle whether you know it or not."

"What's a Focus?"

"That rifle's gonna increase your power ten fold. The fact that you've already touched it is a bad sign. Means I might not be able to reign you in. Frank's not gonna like this. Not one bit."

Things started coming together slowly for Lillian. "Frank's the one that wants me to leave," Lillian whispered.

"At first he didn't think you were too young, and now he does," Annie explained. "Man doesn't know what he wants sometimes. Look, these are dark times, Lillian. We Sharpshooters know what's at risk if we can't recruit to keep our forces strong."

"Strong against what?"

"Demons," Annie said.

Lillian felt her mouth twist. "You're talkin' crazy. Demons ain't real."

"You heard of Paul Bunyan?"

"Yeah."

"Demon. How about Davy Crockett?"

"Yeah."

"Demon."

"No. They were heroes. Legends."

"So the stories say," Annie scoffed. "Demons don't always take human form, mind you. Look, regardless of whether you believe me or not, people like you and I are the strongest line of defense against the onslaught of hell. You may never fight a demon in your lifetime, but if you do, Frank and I want you to be ready to do whatever it takes to defeat it. Bill, apparently, has other plans. He's tryin' to push you too fast and should have damn well listened to me."

Lillian found herself stunned into silence.

"So ya see," Annie said, "I'm not trainin' you to just perform in the show. I'm trainin' you to fight for everything good. And now that your powers have been developed and pushed by that rifle, well, the dark ones will be able to sense you. And demons don't mess around. You're in danger now, Lillian, and . . . it's mostly my fault. And it's Frank's fault too, damn him. He's got a way with my heart. Messes me up. Confuses me."

"You . . . you betrayed me by not telling me what was really going on." Lillian decided that's what it was. It wasn't an emotion she'd felt often; she'd only known glimmers of it from her mother. But that's what this was. Annie hadn't told Lillian what she was getting her into and now it was too late.

"So since we can't get you *worse* so that the demons'll ignore you," Annie continued, her eyes haunted, "we gotta get you *better.* And fast. You don't have time to grow into Lucretia Borgia, we'll have to train harder."

"No," Lillian said, shaking her head. "No. I gotta go."

"Don't be foolish." Annie held out her hand. "I'm

sorry, Lillian, I really am. But you're in a dangerous spot. Too weak to defend yourself properly, but too strong now to go unnoticed."

"Maybe no one will know. Maybe only you know." Lillian had backed up into the tent flap, had her hand on the cord that would release her back into the daylight. "If I believe any of this nonsense about demons in the first place, which I don't . . ." But she somewhat did. Annie had a look on her face that meant she wasn't messing around.

"Your eyes," Annie said. She took a small mirror from her pocket - the very same one that helped her do trick shots - and held it up so that Lillian could look into it.

When Lillian pulled the cord to release the tent flap, the sun flooded in and bounced off of the mirror. She saw her eyes reflected, and where they had once been brown they were now streaked with shimmering orange, like tiny stars were bursting out from her pupils.

"Damn," she said.

"Yeah," Annie agreed. "Damn."

A terror rose in Lillian's gut. "Well, you can't tell me what to do. I'll be safer without you. Without Bill." She threw her old rifle and then Lucretia Borgia to the ground, then turned to go.

"You can run from it," Annie yelled at her as she ran. "But it'll always find you!"

△ CHAPTER 20 △

Lillian lay in the dark with her eyes closed while the Wild West settled in for the night. There were people up at all hours, of course. There were always disreputable characters trolling about, looking for some type of adolescent mischief to partake in.

Horses stamped, men drank, women talked. A few stragglers from the crowd would always be badgering the performers. Maybe some performer had found someone they liked and Lillian would hear them in their tent.

But tonight she was hearing – or at least she thought she was hearing – other noises. The scraping of long, ragged nails. The uneven gait of inhuman legs. Breathing that wasn't quite human or animal. The way Annie had spoken to her, what Bill had done, and what she now knew, haunted her.

Lillian covered her ears, and kept her eyes closed. This adventure had ceased being fun and now she longed for home.

And now she was jumping at the sounds that penetrated her hands, and the shadows that sometimes bypassed her eyelids. She had never seen a demon, but she could picture them: long fangs, red eyes, black skin, claws. She knew she wouldn't sleep tonight.

Something brushed her back and she leapt screaming from the cot, her eyes opened wide.

"Don't do anything rash, Lil," a familiar voice said.

"*Joseph?*" she hissed.

Indeed her brother was standing before her, much bigger than when she'd last seen him a few years ago.

"How did you find me?" Lillian asked. Relief washed over her. After her whirlwind of a day it was comforting to see a familiar face.

"Wasn't too hard once I set my mind to it," Joseph confided. "It wasn't the finding, it was the getting here. Look, I came to take you home, Lil. Father's at his wit's end, and mother's forgiven you. Let's get you out of here. You don't belong here. Can you honestly tell me you fit in with these people?"

"If they want me back home . . ." Lillian started to say. Then she thought of Frank and his eyes and the way he still made her feel when she looked at him from afar. Then she felt foolish. Annie had just told her that something inside was holding her back. She now knew what it was.

And for the first time she realized she had been chasing a dream, an illusion. Frank would never fall in love with her. It was as if Joseph's presence had splashed cold water over her, made her see herself for the young girl that she was. *I'm an idiot. An idiot!* The thought brought tears to her eyes.

She felt moronic. She had convinced herself that her training was the reason she had stayed, but it had always been Frank. She thought back to how she must have looked mooning over him, thinking about him, dreaming about him, watching him all the time.

"I'll go back with you," she said quietly.

"Good," Joseph said, nodding. "The family needs you, Lillian. I've got provisions enough for both of us. You can leave this all behind, we can leave tonight. I can see on your face that it's been rough here." His eyes lingered on hers for a moment, obviously noting the changes to them.

Lillian rose from her bed and began to gather a few things.

"Leave it, Lil. We should get going before anyone notices and puts up a fuss."

"But my rifle . . . I left it in Annie's tent." Her

stomach sank. In her huff she hadn't even thought about it.

"Dad bought you a new one; leaned it in the corner of your room just like you always used to do." Joseph held out his hand. "I'm sorry this whole thing happened, Lil. I'm sorry that mother was the way she was. I think she'll be different now. I think you've . . . beaten her. Well, those aren't the right words. But point proven, Lil. Let's go."

Lillian took her brothers strong, calloused hand and let herself be led out of her tent and into the dark of the night.

$$\triangle$$

This section of the show grounds were unusually quiet and empty except for a few horses that milled about, nibbling the sparse grasses. Joseph stopped just outside of Lillian's tent and grabbed two heavy packs, handed one to Lillian, and turned to leave.

"Hope your feet are up to it," Joseph said as they made their way to the outskirts of the grounds. "Father said I couldn't take one horse, let alone two."

"I'll be fine," Lillian said.

The land became unfamiliar quickly in the dark night. Lillian followed behind Joseph who seemed to be confident in his ability to navigate.

"I think we should be careful," Lillian said shakily.

"Of what?" Joseph asked as he waded through the tall grasses.

"Demons."

"Demons, Lil? Is that what the people at the show have been telling you?"

"Yeah."

"Look, this is part of why mom and dad sent me to get you," Joseph said. "This place isn't a proper environment for a girl to grow up in. Most of the performers are freaks, Lil. Vagabonds, wanderers, drifters. Their ideas are weird. Do you really think there are demons just wandering about?"

"Annie Oakley told me there were," Lillian answered.

Joseph looked at her with a little bit of pity. "You've got to learn to think for yourself, Lillian. If there were demons near the show we'd be waist deep in them right now. Look at this dark night. It's like something out of a scary story. But there's nothing around. We're heading home. Most dangerous thing out here is probably snakes."

Lillian did feel a little foolish. But something warred inside of her. A little part of her wanted to be back at the Wild West, another part wanted to be home, a third part didn't want either thing. She felt the crossroads of her fate coming together. They were only an hour out from the show grounds. She could tell Joseph she had changed her mind, ask him to take her back.

She doubted that he'd be thrilled about the idea, but she teetered on the brink of trying it.

Something interrupted her thinking.

"We've passed this tree before," she said.

"It's just a tree," Joseph said. His voice sounded odd, frustrated. "All trees look alike in the dark."

"We're lost, aren't we?"

"No."

"It's alright," Lillian said. "Don't feel bad, Joseph. We can stop and rest. Try moving again when it's lighter out."

"No, you don't understand," Joseph said. His face was dark, the moonlight turning his eye sockets into deep shadowy caves. "They were supposed to be here by now."

Lillian's skin prickled. The absence of the rifle on her back suddenly became palpable. "Who's supposed to be here?"

Joseph didn't answer. Instead he lunged towards Lillian. She tried to scream but it was cut off by a blow to her head.

△

She awoke lying on her side on the wet ground, her arms bound behind her back. Her head was pounding. She opened her eyes and winced. Everything was bright, but it wasn't day; something about the colors was still muted. The world was was mixed up, backwards: a green moon hung in the sky, the grass was a pale purple, the sky was cream, the mud was crimson.

My eyes, Lillian thought. *Something's wrong with my eyes. Or . . . right with them?* She thought about her irises and how they had looked in the mirror. *Annie said she couldn't coax the power out of me fully. Maybe . . . maybe Joseph was able to.* But she didn't have time to marvel at her night vision.

"You got her far enough away," a gravelly voice said. "We got waylaid. You did a good job thinking quickly."

Lillian almost recognized the voice. She'd heard it before. Somewhere. At the Wild West, maybe.

She twisted on the ground, trying to turn towards the voices so she could see what was happening. A feeling of betrayal lay heavy inside of her. She felt anger starting to build. She had managed to struggle onto her back and now saw a group of people huddling over her, their odd yellow faces looking down on her.

Lillian wanted to shrink into the dirt beneath her, to be sucked into the earth and away from this. She felt her mouth turn into a sneer. *Demons.* She saw their eyes, white-pupiled and wild. *Joseph betrayed me.* Her heart was pumping so hard that she could hear it in her ears. Her shoulders began to burn with blood, the skin stretching. The sensation slowly worked its way down her arms and into her hands, getting under her fingernails, threatening to burst free.

"Hi, Lil," Joseph said.

Lillian stayed silent. She was terrified and furious at the same time. She recognized the group that stood around her. It was made up of various performers from the Wild West. She'd never worked closely with any of them, but she'd seen them looking at her from afar, ogling Annie's new protege.

"You're one of *them*," Lillian whispered to her brother.

"I can't help what I am," Joseph said, shrugging. "And neither can you. It's mostly twins that are born into the duality - one light, the other dark - but sometimes it's not, Lillian. You and I, we're two sides of the same coin. I've known it for longer than you have."

"What . . . what are you going to do to me?"

"That's not up to me," Joseph said. "I'm not privy to that information."

"I trusted you," Lillian shouted. "My whole life I trusted you!" The ropes were hot on her arms. She thought she smelled them burning.

"You said Annie warned you," Joseph said, shrugging. "It's not my fault if you-"

A gunshot tore through the air. One of the demons standing near Lillian fell over heavily onto her, its white blood spurting onto her clothing. She gagged and struggled.

The group standing over Lillian scattered faster than she thought should have been possible, moving with a speed that humans didn't possess. Lillian thrashed wildly, trying to get herself out from under the dead demon. She slid out, sat up, and saw a lone horse and rider streaking around the perimeter of the demons. Her vision was still bright and inverted; she saw everything perfectly.

It was Annie.

Her teacher fired another shot and another demon went down, its skull breaking into black fragments in the night. Another shot rang out and another in rapid succession. The demons were leaping through the night straight towards Annie now, but she was too good of a shot. She felled one after another, her horse dodging bravely through their ranks. It was, very simply, trick shot after trick shot for Annie Oakley.

Another shot rang out and Lillian felt the ropes fall away from her arms.

Then Lucretia Borgia was flying through the air towards her. *Annie was right. I can't escape it.* She reached up and grabbed the rifle from midair. The power in her arms flowed into it and when she stood, sighted, and aimed, she fired the worst shot of her life.

The bullet wasn't operating normally. She could see perfectly so that wasn't the problem, but her shot flew farther than it should have. She'd been compensating for wind and gravity, but the bullet hadn't seemed to be much affected by either one. It had looked like a shooting star.

She marveled at the magic and adjusted quickly. Her next shot rang true, taking a demon in the back. It pierced the humanoid creature and careened out the other side into the demon right in front of it as well. Both fell.

The end of her rifle was red hot at the departure of the bullets.

Lillian felt a new kind of fury wash over her. Joseph's knock to her head must have opened her eyes, and his betrayal had opened her heart. The bullets that flew from her gun were faster, straighter, and more powerful than they had ever been. No demon stood a chance and soon, between Lillian and Annie, there were twenty dead, laying on the prairie in pieces.

Annie rode up to Lillian and reined in her horse.

"We got 'em," Lillian panted.

Annie shook her head. "Not all of 'em. One of 'em had a horse tied up on that ridge over there. I'm goin' after him."

"No," Lillian said, shaking her head. She knew it was Joseph who had escaped. "Give me your horse and leave him to me." Just saying the words made her throat and mouth feel cold, but she had already buried her love for Joseph under a new heap of emotions.

"It's personal, is it?"

"Yes."

"I'm going back to the Wild West," Annie said. "I gotta let Frank know what happened here today; that the show's been infiltrated." The older woman dismounted and handed the reins to Lillian. "Ride down the one that escaped and end him. If he gets back to whoever he's reportin' to, this whole battle coulda been for nothin'."

Lillian mounted the horse and leaned low, ready to shoot off after Joseph.

"He headed dead east," Annie said. "And Lillian . . . you're fully Awakened now. Be careful out there. And again . . . I'm sorry."

"Don't be," Lillian said. "I've got fire in me now and I damn well know how to use it."

With that she sped off into the rising sun, Lucretia Borgia gripped tightly in one small fist.

$$\triangle$$

"So the demon you killed . . ." Whistler said.

"Yeah," Lillian said. "That used to be my brother."

"I'm sorry," the angel said. "The demons work in mysterious ways. As hard as it was, you did the right thing."

"Doesn't make me feel much better. I chased him for more than a week and I thought about what I was trying to do the whole time. There's something inside me now that wasn't there before. A fire that was lurking beneath the surface until it finally broke free. I can see better, shoot straighter. I never miss my mark as long as I've got Lucretia Borgia. Never. For as little contact as I had with Buffalo Bill I wonder now how much of my life was his orchestration."

"It's fate that brought you here, Lillian," the angel said. "You must realize that. Whether Bill Cody knew what he was doing or not, or how much of your story really is his fault, these events are bigger than just him."

Lillian shrugged. "It was love and hate that brought me here," she said. "And I'd like it if we just kept moving and didn't talk about it anymore. I'm not going back home, and as for the Wild West, well, if me and my rifle can be of use to you, Whistler, then I'll keep following you if you'll have me."

Whistler looked at Lillian's eyes, noticing the stars that bristled in her irises, seeing the Fire, the determination, the loss. "Honored to have you along," he said.

Something clicked in Whistler's mind the moment he said it, as if more pieces of the quest were falling into place.

"Three Heroes have been found," the angel noted. "Only one more to go."

▽ PART 4: WATER ▽

▽ CHAPTER 21 ▽

By the tenth day of the journey the sky had blackened and the rain had started. It hadn't shown any signs of letting up then, and indeed it hadn't. The party had now been moving through the rain for five days. Whistler, John, and Lillian, were perpetually wet, cold, and miserable. They hadn't run across any towns since the ghost town where they had met Lillian, and there was no decent cover on the plains. The grasses stretched on endlessly.

The angel's shimmering robe clung to him, revealing the true thinness of his body. "The rain is a beautiful thing," he noted now after what had been several hours of silence. He alone was not irritable from the downpour. Lillian looked like an angry cat, her head covered by a soaking wet blanket. Even John, whose smile always came easily, rode with head hung.

Whistler still couldn't help but linger on Lillian's story and ponder the depths to which the demons would sink to destroy people's lives. He felt them coming for him, even when there were no signs that they were. When lightning split the stormy sky and booming thunder followed a split second later Whistler jumped, but there was never anything there, just like the last hundred times the same thing had happened.

He rode Black. The horse shook his head periodically, spraying water onto the other riders around him. It didn't matter. Nobody could get any wetter. Whistler carried his scythe, transferring it from hand to hand when one got tired of holding it. He had contemplated throwing the heavy, awkward weapon away from time to time, but he couldn't bring himself to do it. His horse and his scythe were the only keepsakes from his farm. From his life.

The ground was squishy, the tall grass the only thing keeping it from being a mucky mess. The four pilgrims cut a line through the landscape, horses trampling soggy grass as they went. The ground was an uneven mess and the visibility was poor; too much so to move very quickly. And even though nothing would have made Whistler happier than getting out of this storm, he and the others held their horses to a walk for fear of charging them into broken legs. The angel seemed perfectly content to be horseless, declining all offers to ride.

"I'd kill for a tent about now," Lillian noted. "Even if it was swarming with demons."

"Be careful what you speak of," John said, water dribbling down off his lips. "We ain't seen one since you joined with us. Don't call them to us now, Miss Smith. This'll pass." The handles of his hammers were soaked, the rain was pinging off of the metal heads.

Whistler wiped water from his eyes and looked off towards the horizon. "Lillian," he said, pointing. "Can you make that out?" A large dark shape loomed, but it was near-black on black, the intricacies of it not visible to him. It was tall, whatever it was.

Lillian flipped the horse blanket out of her face and looked ahead, squinting. Whistler saw her eyes focus, pupils adjusting, irises rotating, whites almost glowing. "It's a tree," she said. "It's a tree! Cover!" She kicked her horse and it started running.

"Lillian, wait!" Whistler yelled after her. A feeling rose inside of him: foreboding, fear. His hair prickled as thunder rolled and Lillian got farther and farther away.

"It's fine," John said. "If she sees something she'll stop."

Lillian stopped.

"Hell," Whistler whispered.

The girl's rifle was off her back in a split second. Wet guns were never good, but Lillian had assured them all that hers would fire. Fire Magic, it seemed, didn't care much about the rain.

Lillian motioned the rest of the party to come forward slowly.

"Somebody under there," she whispered as Whistler caught up with her. "Somebody or something."

"Demon?" Whistler whispered.

"Can't be sure."

The sky crackled with lightning and Lillian lowered her gun slowly. She looked confused.

"What is it, Lillian?"

"It's a woman." Lillian replied. "It looks like she's dancing."

$$\triangledown$$

Even though the storm hadn't let up, the grass became drier as the group neared the tree. Whistler was in the lead where he felt he ought to be. Suddenly he breached an invisible wall where rain no longer pounded down on him. He looked back at the other Heroes. They were still getting soaked, but he was not.

He was close enough to see the woman Lillian had mentioned. She was indeed moving in some slow pattern, almost like a dance. A pillar of clear liquid five times her height undulated next to her, reflecting the lightning flashes.

Water.

Suddenly something was tugging at Whistler's clothing with a million tiny fingers and he became lighter. He watched, stunned, as the water left his clothes, his hair, his horse's mane, everything, and flew through the air towards the woman's moving pillar.

As his companions followed him through the invisible barrier into dryness, he watched their shocked faces as the water flowed from them too. Lillian's hair was revitalized, blowing freely in the wind when she took the blanket from her head. John's hammer handles went from dark to light as the water left them, and the angel's robe shimmered again.

"It's happenin', Whistler," John said. "It's happenin'. Maybe we'll get to the end of this thing quicker than we thought. Praise God, we found everybody!"

Whistler stepped forward towards the woman. "Water Hero," he said to her.

"Sage," the angel whispered to him.

"Sage."

The woman looked up at the party and stopped her movements. The twenty-five foot pillar of water that stood next to her rippled and bent but never fell, held together by some unseen force. The woman had been so distracted that she hadn't noticed Whistler's approach. She didn't appear startled. She said nothing for a moment, but eyed the angel warily. "You travelers?" she asked. Her voice was steady and stark, just like her black hair and eyes.

"We're on our way somewhere," Whistler said. "What about you?"

"I'm on my way somewhere, too."

Lightning flashed. Whistler noticed that once the woman had stopped her dance-like movements, the rain had started to penetrate the area again.

"We're goin' southwest. If it's not too bold of me to ask, is that where you're headed?"

The woman nodded. "Yep. That's where I'm goin'."

Lillian stepped down off her horse. "Then you're gonna need company. Rumor has it there's demons around these parts."

"Lillian," Whistler groaned.

"What? We're gonna be direct with her, Whistler." Lillian turned back to the woman. "This one's an angel. Straight outta heaven, minus the wings. Here's John Henry, maybe ya heard of him. Huge hammers, good with dirt. This one's Whistler. Quiet and slow, but a solid enough fellow. Trusty. Sturdy. And I'm Lillian." She extended her hand. "I shoot demons until they die." The new woman took Lillian's hand. "What are you doin' out here?"

"Practicin'," the woman replied. "Storm came up and I figured I might as well try my hand at this amount of water. Doin' alright with it."

"I'd say so," Lillian said, indicating the impressive pillar of water.

"I'd welcome company," the woman said, "as long you know what you're getting yourselves into."

"We already know," Whistler said.

"Then the name's Kate Shelley. I got a bone to pick with any minion of hell."

"Welcome," Whistler said. He felt the pieces sliding together, locking his destiny in place.

The grass rustled in the wind.

No, Whistler realized. *Not the wind.*

Demons burst through the storm, laughing and screaming, converging on the party from all sides.

Black bucked in fear and Whistler found himself flying through the air. He landed on the ground with a crash. Black turned and ran as Whistler righted himself and recovered his scythe. "Black!" he yelled. The horse didn't listen.

Something horrid was closing in: a pack of demons with insane grins and wicked appendages. There was no time to think. Whistler swung his scythe at the closest demon, the blade singing through the air. The demon jumped back and Whistler almost fell forward. He swung his scythe again, sweeping it along the ground, trying to take the demon's feet out from under it. It jumped and struck out with an arm too long for its body. Whistler brought his scythe up and blocked the arm. The impact shuddered across the weapon and into his body, rattling his teeth.

The demon's arms hit the scythe handle over and over again, scraping along it and sometimes connecting with Whistler's fists, cutting them, the contact feeling disgusting.

We gotta be outnumbered fifty to one. Whistler didn't like those odds, even in the presence of such powerful allies. *Maybe we can run.* There was no exit.

Lillian's shots rang out like thunder and Whistler watched several demons fall. John's hammers were clinking together and then great waves of earth rolled across the ground. The angel was locked in battle with a multitude of creatures.

Something crashed onto Whistler's back and he felt barbs penetrate his skin. In his shock he dropped his scythe. He spun, swinging his fists wildly, and connected with something that made a sharp crack, but as soon he did, another demon was on him.

Whistler shrugged his shoulders and twisted powerfully, like a bronco trying to throw its rider. He pumped his arms and tried to shove both demons away. He succeeded for a moment, but then they were up again and Whistler was roaring at them, furious that he had to fight at all. Suddenly he had a vision of his farm, beautiful and pristine, before the Desolator had ruined it.

He felt a strength come to him that he hadn't known

before. Farming had given him endurance, but this was a frenzy building inside of him. Whistler opened his mouth and inhaled, filling his body with power. The next time the demons jumped on him he released it. Energy surged through his arms. He whirled, his arms encircled with thick barriers of twisting air, and the demons fell for good when he connected with them, torn apart as if they had been passed through a wringer.

What magic was that? What have I done?

Whistler became dizzy, suddenly stumbling, falling to his knees. And as soon as he was down yet another demon rushed at him.

Lillian, John, and the angel were distracted. They would be no help to him right now. Rifle shots, earthen rumbles, and thunder filled Whistler's ears as he gasped on the ground like a fish out of water.

The new demon dove through the air, fully intending to land on top of Whistler and ravage what was left of him, when a ball of water the size of Whistler himself collided with it. The demon folded in the air, and it landed on Whistler as a broken husk, its body ruined.

Kate Shelley stood over Whistler now, using water that she had stored in her pillar as ammunition. She lunged forward and a globe of water separated from the pillar. She clapped her hands together and the water surrounded a demon, crushing it as it gasped for breath. Anything she saw, she felled, and it gave Whistler a moment to recover. He suddenly realized, amidst the chaos, that there was more to his powers than he even knew. He hadn't thought of that before. John and Lillian had both had teachers, guides. Whistler hadn't had one and had stumbled upon his power by accident.

He felt weak inside now, though, hollow as a shell. He figured it to be some kind of magical overload, if such a thing were possible. He couldn't use his power to fight right now; that power would need time to recover from whatever he had done.

Kate and Lillian were standing back to back now, one firing bright orange blazes, the other commanding globes of water. John's powerful arms and the angel's long claws were dealing with an even more sinister crew of fast-leaping, jet black demons. This new, so far unseen breed had no faces as far as Whistler could see.

It's worse than I thought. Not fifty to one, a hundred to one.

While the other Heroes were dealing with the new overwhelming onslaught, Whistler realized he was a sitting duck. Demons were already racing for him. *I need help.* But there wasn't time to Whistle the angel's melody. Everyone else was too distracted to save him this time. *I have to get away.* He Whistled the short call that had summoned Black before, trying to infuse his power into the command. He wasn't sure if it worked.

A pack of gibbering demons rushed up to Whistler, threatening to tear him to pieces, but there was nothing he could do about it. He was unable to fight back. Whistler thought about raising his arms, found the idea too exhausting, and did nothing instead. He'd never feared death, he just didn't want it to happen this way. He didn't want to fail.

Darkness surged in front of him just as the monsters struck. Something huge and powerful slammed down into their midst, pummeling them furiously. It was Black. The horse stamped powerful hooves onto one demon's chest and it stopped moving, then he bit another one's shoulder clean off. The animal's hooves were alive in the night, thrashing and stabbing, cracking carapaces and skulls. The horse - who, up until this point had never injured anyone or anything - fought like an animal possessed.

"You came back for me, boy," Whistler said, relief surging through him. But then he watched the horse fall forward, struggling to stand. "No . . ."

Black fell onto the ground, head thrown back in terror, blood running down his sides. He'd dispatched the demons that had harried Whistler, but now he had paid the price. Whistler felt a rage building inside. He pushed himself up off the ground and gripped his scythe so hard that the wooden handle creaked. He looked for another demon to kill.

"I'll get them for what they did to you," he said.

But vengeance was not in the cards for Whistler that night. Dizziness overtook him instead and the world went dark.

Whistler awakened panting. His arm and leg wounds ached terribly again as he took stock of himself. He was bleeding from his back and the backs of his hands, he still felt dizzy from his overuse of power, but otherwise he supposed he had survived. The demons were nowhere to be seen.

He knew now that he would be useless in any large-scale battle; combat acumen had never been a quality that Whistler possessed, and he certainly didn't seem to be building it now.

And now Black was gone.

Whistler tried to stand solidly and survey the world around him, ignoring the pain he felt inside. He hoped Lillian's keen eyes would spot another attack before it came.

John was feeling the ground again, trying to detect movement. "I didn't feel 'em," he said.

"And I didn't see 'em," Lillian added.

"They're getting stronger," the angel noted. "There are enough kinds of demons that we will never know all of their tricks no matter how many we fight."

"It'll keep gettin' worse, too," Kate said. "I've not yet known it to get better."

"The storm's movin' on," Whistler said quietly, looking up at the sky. "So at least there's that."

"Best to look on the bright side," Kate agreed. She moved her arms forcefully and the pillar of water she had been controlling dispersed and shot off into the distance.

Lillian whistled in amazement.

Kate picked her pack up and shouldered it, then began walking away from the group.

Whistler and the angel looked silently at one another. Whistler wondered if they would need to convince Kate to come with them.

The woman turned around, her dark eyes piercing into Whistler's. "Well?" she asked. "Are ya comin'? I got places to be and I don't wanna be slowed down."

"Looks like we'll be on foot from now on," Lillian said.

Whistler looked around. "You mean . . ."

"The demons got 'em all, Whistler," John said. "I'm sorry."

Whistler sighed and lowered his head. "Then we finish this on foot," he said.

"Looks that way, farmer," Kate said. "Looks that way."

Whistler turned around. "Goodbye, old friend," he said to Black. "I'll see you on the other side."

▽

Whistler was a little shocked at just how much world there was. He'd been cooped up on his property (which he had once thought huge) for so long that he'd forgotten how much nothingness existed. The freedom of his journey tugged him along and helped to remind him that he himself was a small part of everything that swirled around him.

John and Lillian were acting as full-time scouts. Lillian's rifle was never on her back anymore, and John's hammers were always quietly clinking so that he could be ready to unleash shockwaves at a moment's notice.

Even when the party settled down for the night it was begrudgingly. No one relished the idea of sleep, and it was hard in coming. But exhaustion was no real friend to the traveler, and less so to the Hero. Sleep was essential, no matter what nightmare you awoke to.

That night, Lillian was cleaning her rifle, and John was polishing his hammers. The angel sat solemnly as he usually did, doing nothing with his hands for he had no job to be about.

"I'll tell ya about myself if you think it'll be useful," Kate said. "But I'm driven by revenge, angel, plain and simple. You travel with me and it's gonna get ugly."

"I thought I was the intense one," Lillian whispered to Whistler.

"It's alright," Whistler said. "We're all fightin' against wrongs that have been done to us. Wherever it is we're goin', we'll get there together. The angel says we're a full group now."

The angel nodded. "It's come together quickly, which only makes me worry that our mission is that much more important. And that much more dangerous."

"Where'd you come from, angel?" Kate asked. "Just down from heaven to help us out here on earth for a bit?"

"I called him somehow," Whistler said. "I'm wind.

An air Hero . . . I can whistle."

"Kind of a coincidence then, your name," Kate noted.

"Life is like that," the angel said, shrugging. "Coincidences happen often enough that I would think humans wouldn't even accept them as a concept. There are no coincidences. Only fate."

As if on cue, thunder rolled.

Kate looked up at the sky. "Always reminds me of trains runnin' across the rails," she said. She looked down. "Life for me has always been about the railroad. My father made sure of that."

"Your father worked the rails?" John Henry asked.

"Yeah," Kate said. "And if you want to know my story it begins and ends with him."

▽ CHAPTER 22 ▽

Honey Creek was always swollen after the rains of April and May came and went. Overflowing its banks, lapping hungrily at the land, the little Creek seemed to know that it was a tributary of the Des Moines River and was trying desperately to live up to the legacy of those mighty waters.

Kate Shelley sat in the tall grass near the bank, her hair pulled up under a wide brim sun hat, her blue dress buttoned to her neck. She listened to nothing in particular: the birdsongs, insects, wind, and water were her companions this day. And her father. He sat beside her, quietly chewing on a long reed.

A chugging sound began to impress itself upon the noises of the Iowa prairie. It persisted, growing louder and louder. Soon the shining black engine was in view, barreling onward, rushing over the rails with an unstoppable fury that always thrilled Kate.

"She's goin' smooth today," her father said as the train passed. "And people say nothin' ever happens in Iowa."

Kate's father's hands were big as shovels, his arms and shoulders piled with muscle. He'd long been a section hand on the very track the train had just passed over and he always commented on how smoothly it went (if it was "goin' smooth") or how rough it seemed (when it was "goin' rough"). Section hand work was hard on him - Kate could see his tiredness at the end of the day - but a hard man had to do hard work, and besides it made sure that Kate, Margaret, Mayme, Michael Jr., and John could eat.

Kate watched the train barrel off into the distance, its smoke dancing and fading slowly into the air. In its absence, the sounds of the prairie reignited. The birds, the insects, the wind, and the water. Always the water.

Kate stood up and smoothed her skirt. "Best be gettin' back," she said. "Ma's gonna wonder where we are."

But her father didn't rise as he normally would have. It was almost supper time; he was always jumping at the chance to eat. No, today he was in a pensive mood. He stood slowly and looked at Kate. He walked over and put his massive hands on her shoulders, looked down into her eyes.

"I don't know if I've ever told you this, Kate, but I reckon you're old enough to understand. We've got a responsibility, all of us, to this place, to the rails. That section of track that I maintain, well, if I mess it up, people could die. If there's one thing we have to do in this world, it's look out for each other."

The sun glowed behind him. Kate would later look back on this moment and realize that her father was dumping the entire philosophy of his life on her when she was but ten years old.

"Shelleys have always worked hard, will always work hard," he continued. "If we stop workin' we die. That's our lot. That's how it goes. But . . ." Her father paused. "You're the oldest. If somethin' happens to me – and I'm not sayin' it will – but if it does, you help your ma. You gotta take over in my stead. And you protect the littler ones. Make sure they don't know fear, make sure they're strong. I see how you react when the trains go by, little one. You move to watch them like I do. God, I sometimes wish you didn't, but you do. I think you're bound for great things. I hope you're bound for great things.

"So when the time comes to do somethin' great, by God you do it. Some of us have already let our chances go by."

Then her father walked off towards the house leaving Kate shaking where she stood. The gravity of his words and the look on his face would stay with her for the rest of her life.

But her father would be dead within the year.

▽ CHAPTER 23 ▽

When Kate saw the trains after her father's passing her reverence of them was tempered. They now seemed ominous as they approached, huge metal carriages full of corpses, each one going far too fast. She didn't see the grace in them as she once had, only the terrifying inertia.

She had no time to gaze at them anymore, anyway. Her father was dead, crushed by the very metal that he had worked with for so many years, and her mother had taken ill. It left Kate in charge of her four siblings.

This type of life certainly didn't feel like the "something great" her father had talked to her about.

"Michael!" Kate yelled. "I need yer help in the kitchen! Get in here before I tan what's left of your skinny little hide!" Michael Jr. was an appropriate name for the kid; he was a tiny version of his father, and a constant reminder that he was gone.

John and Mayme crashed into the house, fighting and yelling, one of them brandishing a stick like a rifle. Kate snagged John's collar as he passed and yanked him harder than she would have liked. She was strong, her motions precise, and John went toppling to the floor as Mayme began to gloat.

"Come on, Kate," John complained as he struggled to stand back up. "I already told you ya don't have ta tackle me like yer some kinda cowboy."

"And I told you, John, no more fighting in the house. Place is a mess as it is. Good thing you two came in when ya did. I need more wood chopped for the stove." They complained. "And right away!" Kate snapped. She turned back to her baking, her movements swift and sure. Flour, salt, lard, and water flew together in front of her. She

kneaded and rolled, feeling in complete command of the
ingredients if little else.

Margaret came in and began rustling through
shelves. "Mother's fever's up again," she said.

"What's left of the medicine's up there," Kate said,
pointing without looking. "Where's Michael Jr.? We're
gonna eat late again if he doesn't get in here."

"Haven't seen him," Margaret said, standing
precariously on a three-legged stool so that she could reach
the medicine. "Kate, I . . . don't know what I'm doing."

"What do you mean?" Kate asked, transferring the
bread into the oven. It wasn't quite hot enough, but John
and Mayme hadn't come back with the wood yet and there
wasn't much time to waste.

"I mean we can't do this, Kate. We're under water
here. Watching mother day in, day out." She lowered her
voice. "Is she even gonna recover?"

"I don't know how long things are gonna be this
way," Kate said. "Do your best. We're all alive and-"

"We're not *all* alive," Margaret said.

"You know what I mean," Kate said swiftly. She
turned to face her sister. "This is what we're doing, and we
have to do it. We're scrapin' by, but by God we're makin' it.
Now you get goin'. You got yer place in all this. Take care
of ma until I can get us some food. Day at a time, Margaret.
Michael! Michael! Curse that child."

Kate wiped her hands on her apron and went out
back to see if John and Mayme had made any progress with
the firewood. Everyone's responsibilities had shifted since
father's death. Mayme was just plain stronger than tiny
Michael and so she was doing more of the men's chores, and
Michael was Kate's right-hand in the kitchen.

Kate had been planting, harvesting, taking care of
the animals. She'd transformed the place into a ramshackle

farm when she hadn't been allowed to work on the railroad. Taking care of the family wasn't running her ragged, not yet, but she could feel the hands of exhaustion tugging at her. And if she rounded this corner of the house and those two weren't doing their jobs . . .

John and Mayme were fighting on top of the lumber pile, John holding onto Mayme by her hair and laughing grandly while Mayme hissed and spit.

"John Shelley you stop it!" Kate yelled at him, moving swiftly and surely over the piles of broken logs. She'd always been good on her feet, certain of her movements, steady as a stone. She supposed that ability had come from her father. She somewhat shared his build, and he'd been nimble on the rails.

Kate reached the Apex of the pile and hauled John up. She grabbed him by his collar and drew him close to her face. "Get to work," she hissed. "This family isn't gonna make it if you don't pull yourself together and grow up."

"Alright," John said. "Alriiight."

"And where's Michael Jr.?"

"I don't know," John said as Kate set him down. He began to smooth his rumpled clothing as Kate picked up some logs to take back inside.

"Mayme, you seen him?"

"Not lately," the girl said.

Kate got a sinking feeling. Her eyes darted over the prairie. "Michael!" she yelled. No answer.

She heard the rushing water of Honey Creek.

Kate ran inside, a sudden panic overtaking her. She dropped the split wood on the floor and ran to where her mother lay.

"Mom, I can't find Michael Jr. Did he say anything to you?"

Kate's mother had gotten ill just after her husband's death. Her face was thin, her eyes uncaring. The doctor hadn't known quite what to do about it. He'd shaken his head, and Kate had been old enough to know that he'd offered them false hope in the medicine he'd given them. Her mother's thick hair was thinning. She'd lost the will do much of anything at all. Most of Margaret's time was spent taking care of her.

"Michael Jr.?" her mother asked.

"Yes."

"He's around."

"Where, ma?"

"Around," the woman said, waving her hand in the air. Her eyes were distant.

"She's not going to be much help to you today," Margaret said, coming in from the other room. "If you're worried about Michael Jr., go and find him. I can keep things together here."

"Thank you," Kate said. "Dinner's cooking. Don't let it go to waste." She was out the door in a flash.

$$\triangledown$$

Kate ran through the prairie calling for Michael. This country was vast and featureless. Unless you knew it well you were liable to get lost in the never-ending meadow. She wasn't sure if Michael knew it well enough. Kate ran through the dense landscape, through the tall grass that waved, over the rocks that peeked over the top of the water of Honey Creek, and through the tiny copses of trees that dotted the place.

Michael Jr. had his favorite swimming spots in Honey Creek, and they were mostly safe, but Kate knew that on a whim he could be foolishly adventurous. She thought back to the time she'd had to climb a tree to retrieve him from the highest branches, or the time when he had been pressing his ear to the train track as the engine rumbled up.

She didn't see any clothing hanging from branches anywhere near the creek.

"Michael!" No answer. "Curse that boy." Kate was about to turn around and head back to the house when she noticed the bent grass beyond the creek's far bank. Michael had been here, and then gone on farther. Kate could see his path now, at least, and it was recent. "He'd better not be on his way to the Iowa River," Kate muttered as she rushed on after him.

As she walked, clouds gathered and rain fell. Then, clothes soaked, Kate saw something that made her heart lurch. Two more trails joined Michael's original trail, swooping in from the sides. The two bigger trails had certainly been made by two bigger people. The three trails continued on into the distance towards the Iowa River.

"What in the hell . . ."

Kate stepped gingerly along the trio of bent-grass trails, still tracking, but now ready for anything. She didn't know who could have made the other trails. The nearest neighbors were far away. Kate couldn't shake the feeling of dread that was building inside of her.

The banks of the big, rushing river loomed in front of her and still the paths continued on right up to the edge of it. She could see one set of tiny footprints in the mud of the bank, but the other two trails veered off again in opposite directions. Michael's companions had never gone onto the river bank, but Michael had.

Kate looked out over the river. Rain dappled the gray waters. Debris rushed by in the current. Then she saw a dark shape in the center. "Michael!" His body was limp, bent in two, his waist caught on a branch that stuck up out of the water.

Without another thought Kate ran into the water. The currents pulled on her heavy skirts. The further she went the deeper it got and soon she was swimming as hard as she could, terror rising thick in her throat. The river rushed along like a stampede but Kate was determined to reach her brother. The water wouldn't let her. She felt herself being pulled away from where her brother bobbed.

No, I have to get to him.

Losing father had been hard on Kate's family, losing Michael Jr. would devastate what was left.

Kate reached inside of herself for every bit of strength she could muster. Her muscles burned, but she refused to let the water stop her. The rain poured harder. She felt a strange sensation on her arms. She barely noticed it in her panicked determination, but there it was. The water moved away from her. She was willing it away and it was obeying.

Kate didn't know what was happening but she didn't have time to think about it. The water bent around her as she swam violently onward. She shot her hand out and grabbed onto Michael's clothing, pulled herself towards him, and then gripped the branch for support.

Michael wasn't moving, his face was a ghastly gray. He was dead.

Kate strained to free his body from the branch, to untangle his limbs from it. She nearly passed out with the effort, but managed to get him up onto her shoulder.

As she tried to swim back to shore the extra weight was too much. No matter how she bent the water – or whatever it was she had done earlier - she couldn't make any progress. Her head went under and she came up choking and sputtering. She realized that what she was trying to do was insane. The Iowa River would drag her away and she would die just as Michael had.

     She knew it wasn't worth holding onto his corpse. It pained her to let it go, to watch the tiny thing float away upon the mighty water.

     But she did it.

▽ CHAPTER 24 ▽

There were three things that haunted Kate now.

The first was that her mother had worsened. News of Michael Jr.'s death had killed what had been left of her spirit. She now lay, eyes haunted and staring, lips permanently downturned, limbs thin with bones clearly visible. Margaret still took care of her as best she could. Kate would have nothing to do with it. She was obsessed instead with keeping everyone else alive.

Kate knew the story of the ten plagues from the bible and even though it wasn't completely analogous she stayed awake most nights wondering when the next one would strike the people she cared about.

Her mother wouldn't last forever, skeletal and broken as she was.

The second thought that haunted her was the twin paths that had flanked Michael Jr.'s own. Someone or something had walked with him through the grasses beyond Honey Creek. Kate kept listening for whispers when she took her infrequent trips to the nearest town. There were no rumors of strangers in the area, or any mischief. Though Kate had gotten a feeling much darker than mischief from those trails on that day.

The third thing that haunted her was the way she had felt while swimming desperately through the Iowa River. The water *had* bent to her will. At the time it had been an afterthought, but now she wondered just what had happened. Kate knew of miracles, as she was very literate in the bible, and wondered if some greater power had reached out to her, tried to help her. She had failed anyway, even with its aid.

She wanted to call on that power again, craved any

power she could get her hands on, because the stronger she was, the more likely it was that she would be strong enough to intervene the next time something disastrous happened.

And so today, on the banks of Honey Creek, Kate dipped her toes into the water. She'd been able to escape her duties at home for a few brief moments. It had been three months since Michael Jr. had died, but Kate had still felt awful about leaving the house. She felt nauseous when she wasn't at home to oversee everything, but here she was, drawn to the water that held some odd mysteries.

Kate tried to shake thoughts of that fateful day away as she entered the water. She felt it flowing all around her, aware of everywhere it touched her skin, feeling the small currents of this easy part of the creek. For a moment she waited, listening to the quiet nature around her. Then she talked to the water, tried to tell it what to do. Her voice was no use; she hadn't talked the first time, after all. She felt foolish for trying.

She kept trying, though, mixing silent prayers in with her movements. She tried to mimic how she had felt that day, much as it terrified her to do so, and she tried to infuse her motions with that same sense of power and urgency.

For the first few weeks it was no use. All she did was add to her tiredness. Her body complained as she rose each morning, and soon she doubted herself, doubted that it had ever happened. But she clung to faith and stubbornness as her father would have done and one day something changed. In a moment of complete serenity something primal and long-buried swept through her body. She hadn't noticed the sensation before when she had been trying to get to her brother, but every part of her tingled, warm and alive.

Kate found herself blushing and panting as she tried again to force the water to do her bidding. She moved her arms out gently above the surface of the water and watched it react to her motions even though she wasn't touching it. It moved in rhythm with her as she extended one of her legs. This part of the creek was only waist deep so Kate crouched down, feeling the water shock her chest and neck. She spun around slowly on the muddy bottom and again felt the water react to her. She cleared a vacuum around herself - a space devoid of water - and held it for a moment, then the water rushed back in to fill the space.

She was shaking now, not from cold but from exhaustion. Working with the water was draining some different type of energy from her body. She was flexing new muscles. It meant that she had to be done for the day.

She walked back to the bank on weak legs, pushing water from her underclothes with shaking hands. She found that the water flew off of her garments, spraying onto the ground. That simple, accidental act exhausted her even more. She felt dizzy.

As Kate pulled her dress over her head and put her socks, shoes, and hat back on she tried to puzzle out what, exactly, was happening to her. She looked at her hands and arms, inspected her legs and feet; they seemed normal. But brimming beneath the surface of her skin was some type of power, a reservoir of control.

The prairie was quiet today, but Kate didn't notice just how quiet because she was busily absorbed within herself, trying to decide exactly how to proceed with her life in light of her new miracle.

Then she saw them; two figures stood on the far horizon, their shadows stretching unnaturally long across the ground.

Kate stood frozen in fear not knowing what to do. Her house was just a few yards away, but she didn't want the figures to spot her. They could just be men on their way somewhere, but she had a bad feeling. The same feeling she'd had all those months ago.

Kate slowly lowered herself to the ground and crawled the rest of the way to her house. She pushed open the door and tumbled inside, bolting it swiftly behind her.

John was grinding flour near the far wall. "Kate, what are you-"

"Quiet," she hissed at him. "Get down and stay down." Something about the look in her eyes must have gotten through to the usually argumentative John and he crouched low. "Where's everyone else?"

"In the other room," John whispered. "Kate, what's gotten into you?"

"The men that helped kill Michael. They're outside."

John's face turned white. "Are you sure?"

"Yes. Don't ask me how I know, but I know. Warn the others to stay silent. Hide. I have to figure out what to do."

As John went to attend to his task, Kate moved over to the window and peeked her eyes up over the rim. The men were gone. At least, they weren't where she had seen them before.

There was a knock at the door.

Kate dropped to the floor and squeezed her eyes shut. "Just go away," she whispered.

She eyed the gun that hung above the mantel. It wasn't loaded. If Kate was going to risk getting to it – exposing herself to view – she would still have to put in the bullet and powder. One shot wasn't going to be enough for two men.

Another knock at the door, steady and even. Patient.

Don't they realize that I know what they are? Kate thought in a panic. She glanced at the gun again but decided it wasn't worth it. Her body was frozen; where moments before she had felt alive in the creek, she now felt dead.

Her mother moaned from the next room.

Keep her quiet, Kate prayed. *For the love of all that is holy keep her quiet.*

But her mother moaned again, louder. Loud enough that Kate almost bolted in to see if she could keep her quiet. But there was no need.

A tattered piece of paper slid under the door. Kate's hair stood on end.

Writ large on the piece of paper were the words "WE'LL BE BACK".

▽

After what seemed an eternity, Kate got up the courage to move. She grabbed the paper and went into the other room. Her family was huddled together around the low bed where Kate's mother lay.

"Are they gone?" John asked. Usually he looked older than he was, but now he looked younger.

"They're gone," Kate said.

"Who are they?" Margaret asked. "Drifters?"

"They're the men who walked beside Michael Jr. just before I found him dead in the river."

"You can't be sure of that," Margaret said. "They could have just been men that needed help."

"I don't think so," Kate said, showing the paper's ominous message to her family. She watched everyone shrink back visibly.

"That's . . . that's not right," Mayme said.

"No, it's not," Kate agreed. "It's horrifying. We need to keep the gun loaded at all times so we can be on guard against these men."

"They're not men," Kate's mother said.

Everyone turned to her.

"What do you mean, ma?" Kate asked carefully.

"They're demons."

Kate almost wouldn't have believed it. Her mother rarely said anything that made sense these days. But right now her eyes were lucid, she was even propping herself up on her elbows, her thin frame rigid with determination.

"Like . . . demons from bible stories?" Mayme asked in her childlike way, breaking the uneasy silence that had settled.

"Yes, child," Kate's mother said. "Those two men, Kate, were they wearing gray?"

"Yes, ma."

"That's their color sometimes. Not black, but gray." Her mother exhaled heavily. "I suppose it's time. It's probably past time."

"Past time for what, ma?" Kate asked.

Her mother's eyes shifted from terrified to sad. "To tell you kids the truth about your father. You've already realized it about Michael Jr., Kate. He was killed, plain and simple. But your father was killed too. He was something different. Something the demons wanted. Blessed by God."

The children all looked at each other, trying to determine who was believing this and who wasn't. Kate saw a chill running up everyone's spine.

"We're all blessed by God, ma," Margaret said hesitantly.

Mother shook her head. "Not like your father was. He could do things that other men couldn't. He used his powers to build railroad trestles faster than any other rail hand."

"He was strong, ma," Margaret said, not understanding.

But Kate understood. *I am what my father was.*

"That's not what I mean, Margaret. Listen, I need to talk to Kate alone for a moment. Go load the gun, John. Make sure we have enough ammunition and powder. Margaret and Mayme, finish the laundry and cooking. We still have to live even if we're under assault. And make no mistake about it, that's what we are."

Kate's three siblings left the room, leaving her alone with her mother for the first time since her father's death.

"I don't know how long I have," she said to Kate. "I drift in and out. Mostly out." She let a sad little laugh escape her lips. "So listen to me. I can see it in you. It's in the way you move. Just like your father. Strong, sure, in command. Whatever this gift is – God, magic, or otherwise – you've got it too."

"I know," Kate said quietly.

Her mother nodded. "But you didn't know about your father. And now he's gone. He's not here to train you. So here's what I want you to do." Her mother winced and held her hand up to her forehead.

"Mom?" Kate asked.

"I'm alright. Kate?"

"I'm still here, ma."

"Alright. Yes. Once your father began to suspect that the armies of hell were after him, he kept a journal. It's hidden in a compartment on the north wall of the shed. Fetch it. Read it. I'm not sure what it says, myself. It's a side of his life he rarely shared with me. He felt it would be safer that way. But now-" Her mother's eyes changed suddenly. Kate waited for her to speak again, watched her face fall as old thoughts settled back in. "But now he's not around," she finished in a whisper. She was slipping back into her usual self. Thinking about Kate's father and Michael Jr. was too much for her. "Go on now."

Kate scanned the windows, looking far afield for the two men - demons - in gray. She didn't see them, but that didn't stop her from being terrified at the thought of going out to the shed. Kate quickly checked on her siblings to make sure they were alright, then she ran out the door, her heart pounding in her chest.

The prairie looked innocent enough, but now every shadow was a warning, every snapping twig sent Kate looking about. It was a short distance to the shed, and now Kate's hand rested on the latch. She feared opening it, but finally she worked up the courage.

Tools were scattered on the shed's floor: John and Mayme didn't have the same propensity for organization as Kate's father had had. The shed was otherwise empty and quiet.

Kate groped along the back wall with unsure hands, her legs shaking with fright and weakness. There was enough light that she knew the two demons weren't in here, but it still didn't make her feel any less vulnerable. Eventually she settled on a partition in the wood that she could get her fingers under. She pulled and a tiny section of wall came loose revealing a compartment.

Kate reached within and pulled out a small, leather-bound book. A beautiful wavy design was tooled on the cover. *Water,* Kate thought. *Mother was right.*

She began to leaf through the pages, her fear replaced by wonder for a moment. Her father's hand was scribbled and uneven, but Kate could read it if just barely. *No,* she thought. *I mustn't get distracted. I have plenty of time to read this.*

She made her way back to the house to see to protecting her family from whatever lay ahead.

▽ CHAPTER 25 ▽

"I learned most of what I know about myself from the pages of that journal," Kate said to Whistler. She reached into the side of her pack and pulled out the small book. "Still carry it with me. The last remembrance of my father. I've read it hundreds of times. There really isn't much in it, just enough to get me started and keep me goin'. Get the Current flowing, as my father called it. What I can do is Move. Another one of his terms. He says in here that water reacted to him, just as it does to me. There's even a few entries about him and his run-ins with demons."

Whistler found himself shivering. "The demons were huntin' ya," he said. "Yer family. For a long time."

"They were," Kate agreed.

"Why didn't they just knock the door down or break a window when they came to yer house?" Lillian asked.

"My father's journal says that demons may be agents of evil, but he believed they are bound by certain laws, especially the weaker ones. My presence in the home might have caused it to be what he calls a Holy space. That might have been enough to keep them out unless invited in."

"Well then we should all find a home," Lillian said, "and stay inside."

"What about the one that came into my barn?" Whistler asked the angel. "Don't remember invitin' him in."

"A barn is not a home, Whistler," the angel replied.

"I suppose not."

Lillian piped up. "All this talk of darkness is makin' me scared and I don't like feelin' scared."

"We should let Kate finish her story if she needs to," Whistler said. "John, how's the path of the tornado?"

John bent to the ground and placed his palm on it.

"We're still doin' it right," the black man said. "But it's wide and gettin' wider. I'd guess we're gettin' near the end of it, if I'm seein' these patterns right."

"The end of this path will be the end of our journey," Whistler said without knowing how he knew. "Lillian, hang in there. Kate, please continue."

"My powers only kept on growin'," Kate said as the party resumed their wary walk. "I worked with a frenzy after those two demons came knockin'. Almost killed myself once or twice tryin' to gain power, tryin' to learn what I was capable of. My father's journal was right about my presence keeping the demons at bay. I didn't understand at the time. God, I wish I would've. Because . . ." Kate paused. "I'm sorry, this is still hard for me."

"It's alright," the angel said gently, his long fingers resting on Kate's shoulder.

"Well, the years passed," Kate said. "Five of 'em went by, tension-filled and stressful. My mother was still alive, all my siblings, too. Then there was the night when the big storm came. And that was when I finally lost my family."

▽ CHAPTER 26 ▽

The storm grew until the sky was black and Kate feared the worst. The clouds were so thick they looked like a great mass of ink being pushed across the sky. Kate began to worry. She was in tune with water now and she could feel the storm coming, a great energy held within the clouds, a torrent threatening to rival Noah's flood.

It started as a soft patter; the barest of showers.

It escalated quickly.

The trees and grass sagged under the weight as rain poured down for hours. Kate's mother moaned as the storm raged on into the night. At the rate the water was falling the entire prairie would be flooded before long.

Kate struggled out to the stable where the terrified animals were trapped. It was better, probably, to let them fend for themselves. She undid the door and let them out into the storm, knowing that they would drown if left inside. She didn't much like their chances outside, either.

The rain came down in great sheets as Kate made her way back to the house. She struggled with what she should do. In a storm like this her father would have gone to check the rail bridge at Honey Creek, making sure it was intact in case trains came through. Kate didn't like the idea of leaving her home for that long, but she also didn't like the idea of a passenger train crashing and everyone drowning.

She knew what her father likely would have chosen.

Upon her arrival at the house Kate checked the grandfather clock. Eleven pm. The house felt ominous in the long shadows of the lanterns.

Kate went into the room where her brother and sisters were waiting, huddled against the storm. "It doesn't look good out there. I gotta check the bridge," she panted.

"If it's washed out I gotta warn the station."

John looked up at her, his face painted in the light of a lantern. "You're crazy, Kate. Let them trains alone. The men know what they're doin'."

"No," she warned. She wouldn't let anyone come to harm. Not like her father. Not like Michael Jr. "No. Take care of mother. If anything happens while I'm away, you lot are in charge. Don't open the door for *anyone*. Get the gun. Keep it ready. Get knives. Get whatever you can and defend this place."

"But-"

"No!" she said more forcefully. "I have to-"

The distant noise of metal grating and wood splintering ripped through the air.

Kate grabbed a lantern and ran to the door, opening it to the roar of the storm. She'd seen trains go barreling through storms, and she knew engineers were headstrong, always trying to meet their deadline with little thought of safety. She may already have been too late.

The rain weighed her down again the moment she stepped back outside. She had to gasp for breath through it because it ran down her face so vehemently. It was raining even harder than it had been a few minutes before. She sloshed across the ground, using her Movements to affect the direction of the rain so that it cleared a little path in front of her, like the parting of a curtain.

Kate pushed forward, using all the things her father's journal had taught her. She Moved and Flowed with the water and it listened to her. She shoved great volumes of it to the sides, causing it to bend around her while still more and more cascaded down.

Soon there was too much. She waded through the water now. The creek had overflowed violently as the bed could hold no more. Something heavy hit her ankle and

she almost went down. A flash of lightning revealed that it
had been a board.

I'm too late, she thought.

Ahead she could see her worst nightmare. The
bridge wasn't just falling apart, it was completely gone. The
wood and metal that had comprised it were floating towards
Kate. The rails dead ended in the air.

Kate stumbled backwards through the water.
Temporarily distracted in her horror she forgot her
Movements and the water surged around her, grabbed hold
of her, tried to drag her down. Lightning struck nearby and
thunder deafened her.

Kate struggled through the mud, trying to get back
into motion, to feel the flow that had let her get this far, but
she couldn't find it. Moving her legs was difficult, her feet
squelched on the muddy creek bottom.

And then she saw the light.

"No," she said, water getting into her mouth as her
heart sank.

The train was already coming, its headlamp barely
able to pierce the darkness. It wouldn't be able to slow
down in time.

"No! Stop!" Kate waved her sodden arms uselessly.

The great metal beast moved over the tracks, water
flying off it from both sides, mighty wheels eating up rails.
Kate watched as it hit the empty space where the bridge used
to be. It screamed and lurched, engine tipping forward,
roaring into the water, steam hissing angrily. Its momentum
stopped, but the rushing water was tugging on its huge
frame, beginning to slowly pull it down.

But there were no cars attached to the engine.

This wasn't the passenger train, Kate realized. This
was a pusher engine, likely sent to check the condition of
the track. Well it certainly had done that. Kate didn't know

how to go about saving the small crew, but she didn't have to comprehend it, she just had to do it.

I have to save them. Anyone I can get to.

She saw two human shapes clinging to debris, gasping for air in the lightning flashes.

Kate spun a full circle in the flood and it cleared away from her, giving her just enough room to Move. She crouched low and then came up again, pushing the water away, watching it for patterns she could utilize. The great engine was a dark shape below the water now, and the wave it had made was just reaching her.

Kate brought her arms together in front of her face then flung them wide, diverting the wave. It roared around her and she Moved forward again. *Moses was what I am*, she suddenly realized. The thought bolstered her. She was surging forward, legs churning. She reached one of the men and flung her arms behind her, clearing a dry path for him.

"Get out!" Kate yelled over the storm. "Walk out or crawl out if ya have to!"

The man staggered towards the creek bank on the newly cleared dry land.

Kate Moved towards the other man and was able to control a globe of water beneath him, persuading the metal door he was riding on to move in the direction that she wanted it to go. Between holding open the dry path for the other man and moving the door for this one, Kate's mind was full. She almost forgot to control the water that threatened to swallow her up.

She turned, looking for slightly higher ground, and found what she needed. She directed both men to it.

They all ended up on the bank - or, at least, what would have been the bank on a dry day - coughing and sputtering. The men stood in knee-deep water on shaky legs. They were bleeding through their clothing in too many places.

"Who . . . who are you?" the first one asked.

"Kate Shelley."

"God bless ya, Kate. I don't know how ya did what ya did, but we sure needed that miracle."

"Were there more on the train?" Kate asked between lightning strikes. They were her only light now. She'd lost her lantern sometime during the rescue.

"There were four of us," the first man said to Kate, panting. Water, mud, and blood were mixed on his face. "The other two're prolly lost out there." He gestured weakly to the rushing water.

Kate scanned the creek, but there was no sign of anyone else in the grayness.

"Don't worry about them," the second man said. "We'll find 'em, take care of 'em if we can. Kate, you gotta get to the train station. Agar and I are in no shape to do it but someone's got to warn Stationmaster Morris that the Honey Creek bridge is out."

"Alright," Kate said, nodding.

"We can fend for ourselves," Agar said. "Go."

Kate turned and ran, tired though she was. The world was water and she was exhausted. She was almost too tired to navigate her way through the flooded world. Going over the Des Moines River bridge would be the only way to reach the station in time. She stuck to the high ground until she reached it.

The ties of the bridge were wet and slippery and had been built far apart to discourage people from crossing it. *A fine time for that,* Kate thought. The wind howled and the rain pounded the world as she began to cross.

The river coursed below her and she didn't know for sure if she had enough power left to go through the water. She'd never been tested like this yet.

Kate dropped to her hands and knees so that she could crawl across the slippery trestle. Every part of her body was soaked; her clothes were heavy chains. She had to strain her body, reaching forward, stretching her arms longer than they wanted to go and then hauling her legs in once she had a grip on a railroad tie. One tie at a time. Slowly. Slowly. Lightning cracked next to her, threatening to strike the track.

Halfway across she almost gave up. Errant strands of hair were sticking to her face, blocking most of her vision, but she didn't have a free hand to brush them away. She kept pushing forward, letting the work hypnotize her.

Relief flooded through her when she felt ground instead of another tie. She got her feet under her and took off at as much of a run as she could muster. It was still two miles to the station. She knew time was short. If the passenger train came through and nobody had warned it then everyone on board would likely drown.

Kate raced through the storm keeping her eyes fixed on the one small lantern she could now see swinging in the distance. It had to be leading her towards the train station. Her breath was coming in ragged puffs as she reached the building.

The train station roof was pouring rain like a waterfall and Kate burst through it as she tore through the front door, swinging it shut quickly behind her.

It was quiet inside, the sounds of the rain muted for the first time since she had left her house. She stood still, her clothes dripping water onto the floor, her temples suddenly pounding with the painful headache she was no longer distracted from. Her hands screamed with pain from the slivers she'd gotten crossing the Des Moines River bridge. She was shivering too, even though it was warm inside the station. A lantern burned on a table, but there wasn't a soul to be seen.

"Master Morris?" Kate called into the emptiness. The station master was an elderly man whose glasses constantly slid down his nose. Usually he was seated behind the low counter that stood along the far wall. "Master Morris?" Kate grunted in frustration. "Master Morris! The Honey Creek bridge is out! Master Morris!"

She heard feet plodding on the floor, but not at a panicked pace: slow and even. The man who entered the room was not Master Morris.

"The bridge is out?" the stranger asked slowly. His hair was slicked back behind his slightly pointed ears. His eyes seemed to look in two directions at once. He started to smile slowly. "Then everything is going according to plan."

Kate backed against the door. "Oh my God," she whispered. "You're one of them." She fumbled for the latch behind her and finally gripped it, ripped the door open and flung herself back outside. She screamed as she saw the headlight from the passenger train approaching in the distance. She ran towards it, hoping to stop it herself somehow and she tripped over something.

She pushed herself up, knowing that what she had fallen over had likely been the body of Master Morris. There wasn't time. She had to beat the demons. Her father had told her to do something great. *Well, pa, this is my chance.*

Kate harnessed everything she had left and ran towards the oncoming passenger train. It barreled along the track like an iron beast, howling and belching. She knew there was no way the engineer could see her through the blackness, so as the train drew closer she harnessed the rain around her, grabbing as many tiny droplets as she could. She Moved forcefully, combining the droplets into bigger globes, and the bigger globes into a sheet of water, then she slammed the whole thing onto the front of the train as it sped by.

Kate willed the sheet of water to have ropes and she grabbed onto the flailing things and held on tight. She felt her arms almost rip from their sockets as her feet came off the ground and now she was flying, hanging onto ropes of water attached to the sheet of liquid that draped the front of the thundering machine. She was now like a very small kite attached to a giant iron horse.

Kate drew more and more power from the storm around her. The rain began to drench the train, sticking to it as if it were magnetic, an ever-growing blanket. The wheels began to grind against the track under the weight of the water. Kate bent the rain to her will, hanging onto the water ropes with one hand and directing the downpour towards the train with the other. She felt something warm begin to run from her nose and ears. Her eyes threatened to pop from their sockets.

Still the train thundered down the tracks coming ever closer to the Honey Creek bridge.

The power inside was almost too much for Kate, squeezing her heart, choking her breath, but she didn't let up. Lightning flashed and trees crashed down around her as Kate was pulled through the air next to the train. The rain flew from the heavens fully at Kate's command now, coating the train, covering it in a layer that grew thicker by the second. She was careful not to crush it. She just needed to slow it down enough. Even if the engineers had seen that the bridge was out they wouldn't have been able to stop in time.

The gap where the bridge used to be was in sight. Kate screamed, her throat ragged. She started panicking. Calling on the last of herself Kate pulled great globes of water from the ground around her, adding them to her collection. The train sagged and slowed, wheels grinding, the weight of the water dispersed in and around it becoming too much for it to move through.

Kate felt herself fall then. The massive coating of water she had just had control over ran from the train in a tidal wave that washed her away.

All was gray, and then all was black.

Kate's eyes creaked open painfully. The light hurt her head, but at least, as far as she could tell, the rain had stopped. She heard the world dripping dry quietly around her. She tried to push herself up on weak arms, unsure of where she was, but feeling a straw mattress beneath her. Her stomach was twisting with a deep hunger.

"A demon," she panted. "A demon is in the station."

Suddenly she realized that someone was sitting on the bed next to her and she tried to scramble away, but she was too weak. Her body gave out and she was forced to lay back down, terror gripping her.

"It's alright," the man who was sitting on the bed said.

He's one of the ones I saved from the creek. I'm in my own house. But it's so quiet.

"My ma," Kate said.

"She's in the other room, Kate," the man said. "You remember me?" He was leaning over her, inspecting her with a concerned look on his face, as if she were on the brink of death. That didn't feel far from the truth.

"Sorta," Kate said.

"I'm Agar. Adam Agar. I found you half-drowned as I was headin' back towards the station. I carried you here.

The passenger train's been evacuated. The people on it are safe. You're a heroine, Kate."

"The demon-"

"Hush now, ma'am," Agar warned her. "You've been through a lot. Don't get yourself worked up with talk of nonsense. Rest, relax for now. I'll try to get some food goin'."

"Tell one of my sisters to do it. Or maybe . . . my brother."

"Where are they?" Agar asked.

"Should be out . . . in the other room."

"Kate," Agar said gently, "besides your mother and I, there's no one else in this house."

▽ CHAPTER 27 ▽

"My siblings weren't out in the prairie, either," Kate said. She flipped her father's journal around nervously in her hands. "They were gone. Just like that. Vanished."

"The other two men that you never found from the first train," John Henry said. "The ones that Agar spoke of. They were demons. While the storm raged, they took your family."

"Yeah," Kate said. "And you're partly right. But my mother was still in the house. Why wouldn't they have taken her, too? When I recovered enough I went to talk to her. It was hard to understand what she was trying to tell me; she was less lucid than ever. She imparted to me what she could of the events that had transpired. She didn't really remember much, but from her descriptions . . . well, she believed . . . she believed that an angel intervened and took the children somewhere before the demons could get 'em." Kate paused. "Was it you, angel?"

"It was not me," the robed creature said, shaking its head slowly. "But it could have been another of my kind."

"My father's journal talks of a place called the Tannehill Orphanage. It says he'd heard rumors that it was used as some kind of safehouse from the demons. Sort of a place that's immune to their influence. Maybe a Holy space. There are no specifics, but there's enough in the writing that I believe my sisters and brother may be there. And I know what you're thinkin'. And this *is* a last ditch effort for me. I'd almost turned around before I met all of you. But I don't have anything else to go on. My father's journal doesn't mention the location of the orphanage, just that it's in the west. Have any of you ever heard of it?"

"No," Whistler said, looking around. "But things

seem to have a way of working themselves out around here. John wanted to find the machine that cost him his friend. He did find it. Lillian wanted revenge and she got it just as she met up with us. If you stay with us, Kate, you'll find your siblings. I promise it."

The angel nodded his agreement. "This happened to you five years ago, Kate," the angel said gently. "Why didn't you go after your siblings until now?"

"A few reasons. What I did with the passenger train - all the power I used - it broke something inside of me. Wasn't able to Move again for awhile after that. Secondly, I was taking care of my mother. I couldn't bear the thought of putting her up with neighbors or leaving her alone. Well . . . my mother died a few weeks ago. And I can Move well enough again. Nothin' like before, mind you, but good enough to fight. Now's my time. I'm gonna get my family back."

"We," Lillian said. "*We're* gonna get your family back."

"Yeah," Kate said, smiling for the first time Whistler had seen. "I guess I've got company now."

"We're all together now. The melody, the rhythm, the movement, and the emotion," the angel noted.

The four mages looked at each other.

"I guess we are," Whistler said. "I guess we are at that."

• PART 5: DARKNESS •

• CHAPTER 28 •

"The demons have cost all of us so much," Kate said as the party trudged across the grassland. She was in the front of the group, right next to John Henry now.

"But this isn't a new conflict," John said, one hammer resting on each shoulder as he walked. "We know now that they've always lurked among us. We're just not blind to it anymore. And, yeah, they've cost us, but maybe we can strike a blow against them, and soon."

"Perhaps," the angel said. "If that's what this journey is really about. Whistler has set our trajectory, so this all starts and ends with him. The rest of you are caught up in his influence."

Whistler trudged along in the back, feeling the responsibility start to weigh on him. When the angel talked he always spoke of how Whistler was supposed to know what was going on, how Whistler had been the catalyst for all of this, how Whistler was in charge. The farmer felt anything but. He wasn't a legendary steel driver, or a trained sharpshooter, or someone who'd saved the entire passenger list of a train. Nobody had likely ever heard of Whistler.

He'd been gone from the only home he'd ever known for almost a fortnight now. He wasn't sure how far he'd traveled in that time. A hundred miles, maybe more. His travels made him think back to his life before he'd accidentally summoned the angel. He'd had few acquaintances, certainly no friendships. But John, Lillian, and Kate had been instant companions. They'd all been through similar things and had shared their stories extensively with each other over the past few days.

There was only one thing that Whistler had withheld

from them: the tale of his wife, and their inability to start a family. He'd only told the angel that, and didn't plan on letting the story of that sad shame free from his lips again.

On the third day after Kate had joined them another town came into view.

"It's alive this time," John confirmed. "Feet shufflin' all over that place."

Wagon paths led the party as close to civilization as they had been. Whistler heard men shouting to one another, horses clopping, axes striking wood, bells ringing. And as the party approached it, the setting sun to their backs, John Henry bent to the ground, felt it, and said, "I've lost the trail."

"You mean you can't tell which way it went?" Lillian asked.

"No," the black man replied. "I mean this is where the tornado started. There is no more. We're at the beginning of the tornado's path and the end of ours."

Whistler nodded. His legs ached, his body was tired from survival, and his nerves were still ragged from always being on guard against an attack. But now here were people, civilization. Yet some of them, probably, were demons.

So Whistler looked around, saw the determination in everyone's eyes, and decided he'd better play the part the angel had cast him in.

"We're here," the farmer said. "This is the place. Let's show the demons what we're made of."

●

"Yer not from around here, are ya?" one of the citizens asked of the party. He was looking up at Whistler and the rest as if they were visitors from another planet.

The angel, arguably, was, although Whistler was unsure if the man could see him. If he did, he certainly didn't react accordingly.

"We're travelers," Whistler said.

"Travelers plannin' on stayin' or plannin' on movin' on?" the man asked.

Whistler looked to the angel for an answer, but the angel was silent, the look in his golden eyes telling Whistler that things were in his hands now.

"Not sure, honestly," Whistler answered.

"Yer weird," the man said.

"Where are we?" Lillian asked.

"Irving, Kansas," the man replied. "Nice place." He still eyed the group suspiciously. "If yer lookin' fer food you want Sarge's Store in the town center. If ya want ammunition, new heads fer yer hammers, or a new blade for your . . . strange-lookin' scythe, the smithy is along the stream to the west of here. Beds for the night are easy to find. Folks are kind 'round here, and if ya got money or skills, they're even kinder. Some won't take kindly to your freed slave, though."

"He's a good man," Whistler said, looking at John.

"I don't really care," the man replied. "I'm just tellin' it like it is."

Kate stepped forward. "We're really lookin' for a place called the Tannehill Orphanage. Is it around here?"

The man thought for a moment. "Never heard of it," he said finally.

Kate looked back at Whistler and he shrugged his shoulders. The way the man had answered hadn't felt right. It had almost been as if he had half-remembered the place from long ago or far away, but had then decided that whatever recollection he'd had was too unreliable to report.

"Ya'll can have a look around if ya like," the man

said finally. "Don't cause any trouble and we won't put trouble on you."

●

"Am I the only one who thinks that was exceedingly odd?" Lillian asked, once the party was out of the man's earshot.

"And it'll likely get odder," Kate said. "Angel, I don't think that man could see you."

"It didn't seem like it," the angel agreed. "That is what I expected upon coming here, though. Most humans simply won't notice me. Heroes, yes, regular people no. I will seem like a shimmer in the air to them, nothing more than a trick of sunlight."

The town had a strangeness to it that Whistler couldn't put his finger on. He wasn't sure that he wasn't just being affected by the overwhelming crowds of people. As many as ten at a time were grouped together outside buildings, talking and laughing. Horses and wagons moved through the town as well, making navigation difficult. Perhaps there was some way of knowing when and where people were supposed to go, but Whistler wasn't privy to it. He'd gotten so accustomed to walking pretty much wherever he pleased, and now he felt pushed and bumped around by unseen hands.

"I think we should keep checkin' on this place," Whistler said. "There's gotta be somethin' here. I'd be willin' to bet we're in the right town, just gotta find the right spot."

"Do we need to resupply like the man suggested?" John asked.

"I don't know," Whistler said. "Any of you got

money on ya? I don't have a cent to my name right now."

John Henry and Kate both shook their head.

"Maybe we could work for food," Lillian suggested. "Look, it's been fun eatin' rabbits for weeks on end, but I swear if we're about to take on the armies of hell it'd be best if we had some decent grub. I never use bullets anymore, so I don't need 'em. John's got his hammers, and Kate doesn't need much of anything at all. We could maybe get you a gun, Whistler, would be the only other thing."

Whistler looked down at his blackened scythe. "Never been much good with a gun," he said. "I mean I had one, but I never really used it. Missed coyotes nine times out of ten with it. I think I'll stick with what I got."

"Suit yourself," Lillian said. "But we're goin' to that general store and we're gonna get some good food someway. Any arguments?"

There were none.

●

The town center was even busier than Whistler had thought possible. He'd never seen such ruckus. People were shouting and talking over each other, casting glances at Whistler and his party who must have stuck out like sore thumbs.

It made their search for the Tannehill Orphanage easier and more difficult at the same time.

"Wassat?" a man asked Whistler.

"The Tannehill Orphanage," he repeated over the din.

The man shook his head in the same slow way that the first man had. "Never heard of it," he said. "It ain't around here."

"Are you certain?" Whistler asked.

"No," said the man. "But I got things to be about, sir, and so if you'll excuse me."

Lillian came up to Whistler, her hands loaded with all kinds of stick candy. "What?" she asked. "I ain't come all this way to die without some sweets."

Whistler wasn't sure he wanted to know how Lillian had gotten the candy so quickly.

"Control yourself, Lillian," Kate said as she glided by. "You may not know how to handle yourself around people without drawing unwanted attention, but you can take a lesson from me."

Lillian stuck out her tongue at Kate as she passed. "Got any leads, Whistler?"

"No," the farmer admitted. "If the orphanage is here - and I'm almost certain that it is, got a feelin' in my gut - then we're gonna have to find it ourselves."

Whistler felt the pair of eyes looking at him from the corner before he saw them. They had an appraising quality that didn't belong to anyone else from this place. The populace of Irving, Kansas seemed more and more detached from reality the more Whistler walked among them. Where their eyes were shallow, the starer's were deep.

So Whistler walked over to the man. "Yer watchin' me," he said.

"Who wouldn't be?" the stranger asked. A man of sixty, he wore a wide-brim straw hat, a button-up checked shirt, and brown burlap pants that hung just to his shins. He was barefoot as well, which Whistler found odd. A handkerchief was tied around his neck. "Ya got quite the followin'. Even a freed negro among you, and I like that. Them women look dangerous as mountain lions, too."

"They are," Whistler agreed. "We're lookin' for a place called the Tannehill Orphanage."

The man nodded. "A man like you would be."

Knowledge danced behind his eyes. "Well, it's here, despite what these other sleepwalkers'll tell ya. There's a creek that runs a few miles west of here. Follow the waters south and they'll lead you to the orphanage."

Whistler nodded. "That easy?"

"That easy," the man said. "But don't think anything about that trip is gonna be easy."

"I won't," Whistler said. "Do you . . . know what we are?" The angel hadn't said anything about a fifth Hero, but this man certainly would have fit the bill in a different time and place.

"I got my hunch," the old man said. "Think I used to be what you four are, but my time's long done. Listen, I know that orphanage. It's powerful strange. If I was a younger man I'd join ya, but my path lies elsewhere for now, I'm afraid." The old man leaned close and whispered. "Just know that I got a bone to pick with demons, same as you."

"Most people I meet seem to," Whistler said.

The old man nodded knowingly. "Best be on your way then," he said. "There's only so much daylight left, and once the sun sets the curtain of charity gets pulled back from that orphanage and it'll be the demon's turn to hold it again." The old man's eyes left Whistler's and scanned the store. "They're here," he hissed. "You must be a wild group to draw 'em so quickly. Look, I'll distract 'em. You get the hell out and on your way."

The man pulled a wickedly carved slingshot from his back pocket as Whistler turned to go. He grabbed Lillian and Kate by the hands and walked quickly from the store. He would just have to leave it to John and the angel to follow of their own accord.

"Didya figure it out?" Lillian asked.

"Yeah, but demons were in the store. Best not to draw attention to ourselves when we're this close."

"Demons? How do you know?"

Whistler heard a loud sound - like a slingshot stone caroming off of a wall - come from the general store.

"I just know," he said. "Ya gotta trust me." He looked back to see John Henry and the angel running to catch up.

"Is this it, Whistler?" John asked.

"Yeah," Whistler replied. "Follow me and do it quick."

He walked straight west until he found the trickling waters of the stream the old man had referred to, then turned south. The rest of his party followed, wary of attack in the open prairie.

"You sure this is right?" Lillian asked.

Suddenly Whistler saw something glinting at him from the water. The picture of his wife that he'd had the angel toss in the stream near his farm all those weeks ago was floating in the water, bobbing merrily along the currents.

Whistler's hair stood on end.

"If ever there was a sign," the angel said, "that's it."

The photo rushed down the stream and Whistler followed it. He scrambled through briars and over rocks that threatened to trip him. He nearly fell several times but caught himself on his scythe, using the black, twisting object like a crutch. By the time he lost sight of the photograph he was breathless.

It was then that he saw the orphanage.

• CHAPTER 29 •

Whistler parted the foliage and peered out at the building in the distance. The words "Tannehill Orphanage" were engraved on a sweeping piece of metal scrollwork that ran above the rusty gates. People passed, walking on the worn paths of the small town, but none of them looked at the orphanage for long. Each passerby, if they looked at it, seemed to suddenly remember to look elsewhere.

"Something - either holy or demonic- has a Guile on that building," the angel said. "Notice how the people look away from it as if they refuse its existence."

"My family," Kate said, shuddering. "If they're in there, angel, we'd best be quick. I don't like the look of that place one bit."

"There," Lillian said, pointing.

Whistler hadn't noticed it before, but as he followed Lillian's finger he noticed eyes in the bushes that sat to either side of the big gate. They were human, but strange - just like Whistler's companions had described them - pointing off just slightly to either side. He'd not seen a human demon yet, but he knew that he had now. A chill passed through him.

"Guards," John whispered. "They want to keep us out."

"Or they can't get inside," Kate said. "Remember, if that place is Holy they might not have the ability to enter."

"I can shoot 'em in the pupils from right here," Lillian said, pulling Lucretia Borgia from her back. Whistler watched her cheeks flush and her pupils dilate.

Kate stopped her. "Don't act rashly, girl. We don't know for certain what we're up against."

"We're up against demons," Lillian said. "And I'll

kill every one I come across." Her gun sang, meteoric bullets drilling right into their targets.

Whistler's heart dropped.

"Fire Heroes," the angel said to him, shrugging. The tall white creature burst from the foliage and ran towards the gate, John hot on his heels, hammers already clanking. Kate shot out, moving low to the ground. The nearby stream reacted to her passing. Lillian whooped and leaped out, sighting the windows of the building in a flurry. And just like that Whistler found himself alone and struggling to keep up with his frenzied, excited companions.

Something felt wrong to him as he shifted his bulk and started to run. The passerbys who had been so complacent now seemed to notice everything around them. They began to scatter like sheep. The grounds around the orphanage came alive, deformed creatures rushing around the sides of the building.

A demonic alarm had been sounded, and everything was answering its call.

Whistler ran forward, trying to concentrate on a hundred things at once. It was too much.

John Henry had met the front line of demons. They were small, agile, and swarming like eager insects. Barbed limbs and large mouths with too many teeth tried to descend on John, but the Forger was too powerful. His hammers sang through the air, their clinking rhythm interrupted only by demon carapace. He felled more and more, his black arms glowing in the sunlight.

FOOM! A great gout of earth flowed forth from him and upended the rusty gates, toppling them backwards onto the next group of demons, crushing them, snapping arms, legs, necks.

Whistler lurched forward and swung his scythe at the chest of a demon. It connected, crunching, but the demon swung its arm as it fell and was able to rake a gash into Whistler's arm. Whistler was so shocked that he dropped his scythe. When it hit the ground it cracked in half.

Whistler screamed and punched downward, catching the demon in the face. It scrambled backwards.

With nothing to defend himself, and a small window of time to react, Whistler put his lips together and quickly blew the melody that would call the angel to him. The white being shot in front of Whistler in a beam of light and struck out. The angel's hand disappeared swiftly into the demon's chest and ripped out its disgusting heart.

The demon - which had been reasonably human - had a surprised look on its face as it died. Then the angel was dancing away again, its gold blood mixing with black.

Whistler quickly retrieved the larger piece of his broken scythe. If it had been an awkward weapon before it was even more awkward now. It was little more than a short spear, its five foot range reduced to two. Whistler couldn't quite figure out how to hold it. But as he was fidgeting with it something caught his eye and he saw what the others didn't.

A Desolator, like the one that had stood atop Whistler's barn what seemed an eternity ago, now stood on top of the orphanage's tall, sloping roof. It began to open its mouth, to howl and create a wave of death.

"Lillian!" Whistler shouted, trying frantically to find the Sharpshooter in the chaos. He couldn't see her, but he could hear her gun. "Lillian!"

"Whistler, what is it?!" the girl shouted between her gunshots. He saw her then, blond hair flying in the wind, black blood covering her from neck to knee.

"On the roof! You've got to take it down!"

Lillian swung around and sighted, but just as she pulled the trigger a demon crashed into her. Her meteoric

shot went wide, the Desolator still untouched and proud
atop his throne. Whistler grunted and raced towards Lillian,
trying to reach her before she was killed by the demon that
now pinned her to the earth.

Whistler stabbed with his broken scythe and the
blade sank into demon flesh. The demon howled and dove
off of Lillian, gripping its side and chittering angrily.
Lillian was hissing and spitting as she scrambled to her feet.
Again she swung towards the Desolator, aimed, and pulled
the trigger.

Nothing.

"John!" Whistler shouted. There was no time to
figure out what was wrong with Lucretia Borgia.

Whistler ran towards the man with the silver
hammers, ducking under the swinging arm of an advancing
demon.

"I see it, Whistler," John said. Black and green blood
spattered his clothing. "Keep 'em off me."

As Whistler raised his stub of a scythe defensively,
John raised a hammer over his head. The Desolator began
to wail and Whistler knew it wouldn't be long before the
world was engulfed in a ripple of death.

"Come on, ya bastards," Whistler said to the demons
that were now running at him. "This is where my adventure
ends, one way or another."

Whistler stabbed, lunging forward, and caught the
first demon through the neck. It fell but didn't die.

One of John's hammers was careening through the
air now, flipping end over end. Just as it reached the
Desolator, the thing jumped to the side and the hammer
whipped harmlessly past.

Whistler cursed and kicked out at another demon,
knocking it off its feet. Whistler brought his lips together to
summon the angel and suddenly something caught him in

the face and he reeled backwards, pain blossoming from his mouth.

Whistler was spun around, and as he whirled he looked up at the Desolator and saw that John had been a step ahead of it. The Forger's second hammer was already sailing towards where the Desolator had dodged to. The flying whirl of metal and wood connected with the Desolator and carried it off the roof with a mighty, crunching thud.

And John was fighting again, stomping the ground. Demons screamed as the earth ate them up, their bodies crunching beneath undulating waves of soil.

"We have to get inside!" the angel shouted over the rumbling. Whistler had never heard him shout. His voice didn't sound any more strained, just louder. "Whatever they're guarding in there, they'll stop once we claim it! They'll be recalled back into the darkness to suffer for their failure!"

Kate was already at the door struggling to blast demons from the rickety, rotting porch and gain access to the place that she was certain held her siblings. "If we're gonna go in, let's go in!" she shouted. Her body moved fluidly and water rushed from a nearby barrel, summoned forth to crush the last two demons in her way. Just as she laid her hand on the doorknob another demon dove towards her and struck out with long fingers, catching Kate's leg and spinning her down to the hard porch boards. She landed with a loud thump then she scrambled away, limping.

Whistler looked towards Lillian. The girl was cursing at her gun. She flung it to the ground and leaped forward just as a demon's long twisted claws careened through where her head had been. Lillian had a knife in her hand and she jabbed out with futility, suddenly looking every bit her young age, transformed from a fearsome fighting force into a cornered little girl. The angel dispatched the demon that harried her, his claws tearing its chest open and pulling out the heart in one swift, now-practiced motion.

Whistler didn't like the angel's suggestion of going inside the orphanage. Something about running into the very place that probably held the most powerful foes seemed wrong. But in the chaos, with demons closing in on all sides, he couldn't come up with another option fast enough. So he turned and ran, blood pumping loudly in his ears. His lips were starting to swell painfully from where he'd been hit in the face.

My magic. He tried to Whistle, but couldn't. The flesh wouldn't take the proper shape.

John's hammers are gone, Lillian's gun doesn't work, and Kate's leg's been damaged. We're being disarmed, Whistler realized. *It's only the angel left. We can't keep fighting like this.*

Whistler saw demons running towards him from all sides as he pounded up the front steps of the orphanage, grabbed Kate around the waist, and hurtled through the door. John Henry and Lillian followed.

"Angel!" Whistler shouted out the door. His white-robed companion was still outside trying to hold off the horde of demons by himself. "Angel! Get in here!"

The angel whirled and ran, diving through the door. Whistler slammed it, then quickly tipped a large wooden cabinet in front of it.

The horrifying sounds of the outside were muted, and when Whistler finally gathered himself and looked around he noticed that the inside of the orphanage wasn't as sinister as he'd first expected it to be. There was no one inside but the four Heroes and the angel.

"Mayme!?" Kate shouted, her voice echoing through the orphanage. "Margaret!? John!?" Her hair was unbound and flowing, her dark eyes piercing. Her wounded leg was covered in blood and she limped on it.

"Why ain't the demons comin' in?" Lillian panted.

The angel looked around. "This isn't their place." He paused for a moment, looking pensive. "There's something in here that's blocking their passage. Something Holy, like what I suspect Kate told us about. They have it surrounded, but that's as as far as they can come without an invitation."

"No one invite them," Lillian said sternly.

"Are we supposed to hide in here until they go away?" Whistler asked.

"What do you *feel?*" the angel asked him. "You were the first. This is your quest. What is *here?*"

Everything inside of Whistler contracted. He searched inward, trying to have the answers that the angel needed him to have, trying not to let his companions down. His mind was blank and overwhelmed all at once. He tried to rummage through his thoughts, pull some sort of divine idea from them, but he couldn't. He looked at the meager decor of the orphanage. There was no inspiration there. He didn't see or hear anybody else. If this indeed was some sort of safehouse it appeared to be empty for the moment.

And then something came to him on the air. *Of course*, he thought. The faintest of smells hung in the orphanage. He smelled *her.* His hair stood on end again. *It can't be. She can't be here. Doesn't make any sense.* But it was right. Everything screamed it now.

Whistler sighed, finally knowing. *What else would I ever have quested for?*

"It's her," he said slowly to the angel. "The woman from the photograph. My wife is here in this place."

Whistler crept through the quiet halls of the orphanage, the other Heroes behind him. Kate had long since stopped shouting for her siblings when there had been no answer.

Every now and then Whistler would see demonic eyes peeking in through boarded windows. He met their gaze defiantly until he forced himself to look away. But every now and again there was a window that stood unobstructed. The demons were just standing outside in a thick huddle, their faces pressed against the glass. And all of them staring, staring.

It was a horrifying scene. Apocalypse. Every portal was jammed with death. There was no going back outside, for that would mean the end. The orphanage was completely surrounded, pressed with a thick layer of monsters. The scent of Whistler's wife drove him on. It was her hair, he decided. It had always smelled like grass and sunshine.

The interior of the orphanage seemed much larger than the outside had let on. The layout didn't make sense. Hallways twisted and turned and the building seemed to shift around them, and still Whistler followed the scent. The group traveled an impossibly long distance, the silent demons outside simply looking in, unable or unwilling to act.

"How come ya never told us you had a wife, Whistler?" John Henry asked.

"It didn't seem important."

"Seems mighty important now," Lillian said. She was scratching at her hands, first one then the other. "The hell are we goin'?"

"Only Whistler knows," the angel reassured her. "Trust him. Remember that not even I know what truly lies ahead. I am a guide. A confidant. Nothing more."

"I'm not sure we should be in here," Kate said. "Now, I've got courage aplenty. I'm just sayin' if we were smart we never woulda rushed this place in broad daylight." She was still limping, her black shoe now red with blood. "Feels wrong not to have a plan."

"The demons are stronger at night," John said. "This was probably the best shot we had, as much as I wished we woulda discussed it first. But doesn't it feel good, Kate, after all the demons you've seen, to finally be doin' somethin' that'll make 'em think twice?" He put a hand to his heart. "Whistler's journey is all of our journeys now."

The orphanage's hallways twisted and turned without any reasoning. Whistler could feel the magic of the place working, guiding him down one last path.

He came to an open staircase that led down into darkness. "You sure this place is Holy?" he asked the angel, teetering on the top step, unwilling to go down.

"I'm certain," the angel said. "If this is where you feel you should go, this is where you should go, Whistler."

The steps were tall, misshapen. Each step down jarred Whistler, but he knew, somehow, that he drew closer to his wife. He was both excited and terrified as he descended the staircase. Then his mind caught up with him.

How am I going to explain things to her? Should I even tell her about the farm? Our farm? Gone now. Everything we worked for. What was the point when it's all been swept away so easily?

Another step.

He started to become self-conscious, suddenly realizing how much he'd let himself go over the three years

since she'd been gone. Now he was injured as well. Weak.
His arm and leg still ached from the initial attack those
weeks ago. He was tired, bloody, filthy, his lips had to look
frightful. Suddenly, Whistler didn't want to be seen.

Another step.

Is she even still my wife? He'd never stopped
thinking of her as such. They hadn't broken their vows.
The sentiment lay, an eroded pile of words and memories in
Whistler's mind. They'd never worn rings like other couples
did. On the farm it was a liability. Snag it, lose a finger
most likely.

Another step.

A door.

It was hard to see in the near dark, but Whistler
could have sworn that the doorknob he reached for was
inlaid with green gemstones. It was smooth and cold in his
hand as he turned it. The door opened without complaint.

The room on the other side was lit with candles.
Whistler's boots clicked on the stone floor as he entered it.
He heard his companions slide carefully into the room
behind him. At first Whistler saw nothing, fearing his
journey might come to its conclusion in a dead end.

"The candles are placed in a Warding Pattern," the
angel said quietly. "There is something powerful here." His
golden eyes held a hint of worry.

Then Whistler saw her in a dark corner. Shadows
shrouded her. She was crouched, holding something.
Whistler saw her hair, brown speckled with gray. Her
clothing was modest, clean.

"Who's there?" she asked, her voice trembling.

"Emily," Whistler said. "It's me."

His wife stood slowly and walked carefully towards
him. "It's really . . . it's really you? This ain't some demonic
trick? How can it . . . No." Her eyes focused. "No!" She

pulled the bundle she was holding back defensively. "There's one with ya!" She pointed at the angel, her hand shaking.

Whistler looked behind him, a sinking feeling in his gut. "Naw," he said. "Emily, he's . . . an angel."

"Oh, Whistler, ya don't know what you've done," Emily said. "All of the years I've been runnin', with everywhere I've been." She was shaking gripping the bundle in her arms fiercely.

"Now calm down, ma'am," John Henry said. "I know he's covered in their blood and he's got them claws, but he's no demon." John looked at the angel.

Kate moved defensively in front of Lillian.

"My demonic brethren can be such short-sighted, stupid brutes," the angel said to Whistler. "But I actually do feel a little sorry for you, Whistler. I liked you."

Then the room became chaos.

●

The first thing Whistler did as the angel - demon - slashed out with its claws was to dive for Emily, hoping that he could get her out of this place. He grabbed her with one arm and swung her wide, past the candles towards the far wall, trying to buy time.

He turned to watch the demon slashing at Kate. It moved so quickly that its robe made sharp snapping sounds, demonic blood spattering off the garment onto the floor, walls, and ceiling. Lillian ran and grabbed a candle as Kate cried out in shock. The demon had slashed her other leg and the woman sank to her knees.

Lillian rushed the demon's front as John came from the back. The steel driver's massive arms closed around the demon. Lillian snatched a candle from a holder and ducked low with it, trying to get the flame onto the demon's robe. Throwing it would extinguish it; she had to get in close and she knew it.

But the demon broke John Henry's grip like the black man was made of twigs, and again its claws raked out, slicing through the candle and most of the way through Lillian's arm. She screamed and grabbed her wound, trying to keep her blood in.

The demon whirled and John Henry grabbed a tall brass candle stand from the ground. He didn't even have time to tap a rhythm before the demon had cleaved the candle stand in half and laid John Henry low with a mighty swipe across his chest.

The demon turned and ran towards Whistler and Emily next. They'd barely had a chance to move at all.

This is it. At least . . . at least, what?

At least I saw her again.

Whistler raised his broken scythe, but in the blink of an eye the demon knocked him over, then toppled Emily, and then snatched the bundle she had been holding. Whistler's head hit the packed dirt floor and he felt his skull shudder.

The demon was running across the room with the bundle, back towards the door with the green-gem doorknob. He neared Whistler's companions who lay huddled together trying to tend each other's wounds.

"Don't kill them," Whistler managed to say through his broken lips.

The demon turned. "I can't, unfortunately. You all have been my Guides. I need you alive for a little while longer so I can leave this place. Do be helpful and bleed out for me eventually though, won't you?"

"Damn you," Whistler said.

"Yes," the demon agreed. "To hell, in fact." Then he

turned and ran from the room.

The last sound Whistler heard was that of a small child crying.

The bundle that the demon now carried.

A child.

No.

Whistler propped himself up on his elbows. His world spun, but he managed to get to his feet. He gripped what was left of his scythe in two hands, holding it forward like a spear.

"If I can't go ta you," he said, "you're comin' back ta me."

He brought his lips together and tried to blow. A bloody spray. His lips wouldn't work, couldn't form. He tried with his fingers in his mouth. It was excruciating. Still nothing. He re-gripped his scythe with his blood-soaked hands.

I am wind. I am air. What did the angel say I was? I am . . . melody.

His mouth was ruined, but not his throat.

Whistler sang.

He'd never done it before, not really. The notes burst from him as he tried to picture how the angel had always flown to him when summoned, how it had been holding the child as it had fled.

Whistler finished singing the melody.

There was a blinding light and the sound of a thunderclap and the angel - the demon - now stood in front of Whistler, a shocked look on his face. The blade of Whistler's scythe was buried deep in the demon's heart, inches above the bundle that was the child. The demon's shock twisted into rage as it fell. Whistler let go the scythe and reached for the child, transferring it safely into his arms.

Whistler watched the demon take its last breath. It

curled up like a plant withering in the heat and moved no more.

The orphanage began to shudder and twist, boards warping and morphing, dust falling from seams. The cellar room was shrinking. The form of the place was changing as if on cue. A window formed on the far wall along with a new door which grew from the wood, its new red molten knob swirled into place and then cooled to gold.

Sunlight flooded the cellar and Whistler had to blink, his eyes watering. No demons waited outside. For all he could see, the grass had never even been disturbed by fighting. *How much of this whole journey has been illusion?* But his friends were hurt, that much he could plainly see. Their blood, which had been dark before, glowed in the new light, and Whistler was shocked at how much there was.

Whistler cautiously handed the child back to Emily. In the back of his mind, behind the angel's betrayal, behind the feeling that the journey was over, behind other intuitions not fully dredged up, he wondered if the child was his. He couldn't ask. He knew that even if he wanted to, the words wouldn't come out just now.

John Henry was tearing strips of cloth from his shirt and winding them around the ruins of Kate's legs and Lillian's arm. He ignored his own wounds even though blood ran in rivers down his front.

Whistler kept a wary eye on the demon's corpse. It was hard to think of his companion as that, even now. The creature he had come to trust had betrayed him. It lay crumpled, robe still shimmering, golden eyes open and staring at the ceiling.

"The hell just happened?" Lillian asked weakly as Whistler limped over to her and the others.

"We all got taken," Kate said. She grimaced as John

cinched the tourniquet tight.

"Yeah," Whistler agreed. "When this all started I thought I was goin' crazy. I'm still not so sure I'm not."

"She's got the pieces of the puzzle, maybe," Kate said, pointing to Emily and the child. "Is that little bundle what we were after this whole time?"

"It's what your demon was after, anyway," Emily said.

"What's so important about her?" Kate asked. "I mean, she's cute and all, but . . ."

"There's power in her," Emily answered. "Like there's power in all of you. But she's something more." She looked down at the child. "Something I don't fully understand. Look, it's all very complicated and I'm not sure how much time we've got or what happens next. I was supposed to be meeting someone here. They didn't show up."

"I showed up," Whistler said.

Emily smiled. "That might be good enough," she said. "Might be good enough."

"What's next?" Lillian asked.

"Well, Whistler's always led us," John Henry said. "I don't think the angel was lying to us about that at least. So, Whistler. What do you feel? What's our next move?"

Whistler thought. The angel had told him he was a Venturer; someone who longed for travel. He'd felt it himself, bought into it. But now something took hold of him, and he felt only one overwhelming sensation.

As he looked over his battered companions, his wife, the child, he had the overpowering feeling that he just wanted to go home. He knew that that probably wasn't possible, though. He'd seen the Desolator's wave of death and destruction, remembered what it looked like. He would have bet a large sum of money that it festered, too.

"I don't know," he said honestly.

"I guess I might a little," Emily said. "That door that opened here - that's a Portal. Means this room is sealed and that's the only way out. It'll deposit us all back where we belong."

"How does it know where we belong?" Lillian asked.

"It knows."

Kate limped over to the window and looked through. Her eyes widened and tears began to run down her face. "My family's out there," she breathed. "They're alive. Somewhere. This door'll take me to them?"

"What you see on the other side is where you'll go, young one," Emily answered.

Kate turned around. "I have all of you to thank for this. I couldn't have done this alone. Thank you. Thank you from the bottom of my heart. If you ever need me again I'll be ready. I owe you a debt that I might never be able to repay."

"Goodbye, Kate," Whistler said. "The debt's in your favor."

Kate grabbed the newly-formed knob and turned it. The door opened to blackness but Kate must have seen something else for she ran through it with hopeful eyes, wounded legs and all. It shut behind her of its own accord.

"She might have somethin' to get back to but I don't," Lillian muttered. "Where's my happy ending? Lucretia Borgia: broken by demonic idiots. Brother: murdered by my own hands." She approached the window and looked through. "Well. Maybe it won't be so bad."

"What do you see, Lillian?"

"The Wild West," the girl said. "The place could be full of demons. I guess that's as good as anything. Maybe . . . maybe I can try to set that place straight. Mend some of the hurt that's been done there. I'll get to work with Annie again, at least. Even though she's the one that helped curse me like this." A dark look passed over Lillian's face for a split second. "See ya later, Whistler. It's been . . . well, not fun, but it's been somethin'."

"Goodbye, Lillian. And good luck."

Lillian opened the door and stepped through into the darkness. It swung shut behind her.

John Henry was in rough shape as he approached the window. The demon had a gotten a good swipe at him and he hadn't seen to himself; Whistler wasn't sure why he hadn't. But John looked old where Lillian had looked young. He looked like a man ready to be done.

"What do you see?" Emily asked John.

"I don't know," John Henry said. "But it sho is beautiful. Whistler, I think my part of this journey is done for good." He looked from Emily to Whistler. "Take good care of each other now. Look, I don't know what happened between ya, but I know ain't nothin' I wouldn't give to see my friend Abel again. Don't waste what ya got." He gave them both a nod, his blood running into pools on the floor around him.

"Goodbye, John," Whistler said. "They don't make men like you anymore."

"Yeah they do," John said with a slight chuckle. His eyes fixed on Whistler's. "They just don't always make 'em the same color."

Whistler watched as John Henry - a man who it had taken only a short time for Whistler to admire deeply - slowly turned the knob and stepped through the door.

"Well," Whistler said with a heavy sigh. "I guess that just leaves us."

"Yeah," Emily said. She paused for a moment. "What do you see, Whistler?"

Whistler approached the window and looked out. He saw a prairie, much like any other. It was dotted with buildings: a house, a small barn, a pig run, a chicken coop, a storm cellar. It looked a lot like his old farm, but it wasn't.

"Looks like a farm I don't recognize," he said.

"Does it have a picket fence?"

"Yeah."

"And a couple wagon wheels leaned on either side of the barn doors?"

Whistler squinted. "Yeah."

"Then I think we're goin' to the same place," Emily said. "My place in Kansas." She patted Whistler on the shoulder, just like she used to do. "See ya on the other side."

She opened the door and walked through it with the child, leaving Whistler alone in the basement room.

He stood for a moment, taking it all in. *It could still be a dream*, he thought. But he figured that he was best served to treat it like it wasn't. He'd just been on the journey of a lifetime, the kind of trip that a real adventurer would have longed for. Someone stronger might have reveled in it, but Whistler had merely survived it. He took stock of himself, making sure he would be ready for anything on the other side.

When Whistler stepped through the door he felt a power wash over him that tugged at every fiber of his being. He knew that he was slipping through spaces that men usually did not tread. It felt comically fanciful, almost unreal, but the ground was indeed firm under his feet when he stepped onto it.

He turned around and looked back through the door, which stood on the ground in an invisible frame. The empty cellar room stared back. He knew that he probably should have felt more sadness, but the fact that Emily was with him overtook everything else. And so, as Whistler closed the door slowly he felt not an ending, but another beginning.

• CHAPTER 30 •

The door winked out as soon as Whistler closed it.

The Kansas wind was not so much different from the winds of Nebraska, and it blew through Whistler's and Emily's hair as they stood motionless, looking at the farm. The sun was nearly set and the farmhouse stood in the shadow of the barn.

"This where you've been all these years?" Whistler asked.

"Yeah," Emily said. "Everything looks to be as I left it. I hired on three good hands to watch the place when I had to leave. But this is our place to keep now, I suppose. This is where our destinies have led us."

"You mean you think . . . we can fix us?"

"Don't know," Emily replied. "But when I look at you now, Whistler . . . I don't feel like I did all those years ago. Maybe startin' over wouldn't be the worst thing."

"Then let's get goin'," Whistler said, smiling. "Your cow ain't gonna milk itself." He started walking towards the house, stub of a scythe held in his hand, feet shushing through the tall, untamed grasses. He heard the child fuss a bit in Emily's arms and Whistler felt his curiosity brimming, but he knew that once they got inside, and once they made a fire and set up a place for the child, he would get his answers.

●

"So she's not mine," Whistler said as he looked down at the sleeping girl child. She was almost two years old, quite small for her age, but with long beautiful lashes, and a mass of auburn hair on her head that was held in place with ribbons. Whistler felt a bit disappointed. He wouldn't have minded if she were his.

"She's not yours," Emily agreed. "But she's not mine, either."

"Does she know you're not her mother?"

"Yeah, she knows. I couldn't tell a lie that big to her so I told her I was her aunt. She can't say Emily. Calls me Em."

"Where did she come from?"

"She was entrusted to me, and I'm takin' it very serious."

"Entrusted by who?"

"A man named Marvelle," Emily said. "Talked of angels and demons just as you do. If your journey was any indication, I don't think this is over. Not yet. Maybe you're finished, but *we're* only just beginning."

Whistler looked up. "Don't give me grief, Emily."

"I mean it. You had your journey, and I had mine. And now we have ours."

"So when you left before . . . Was it because of this secret journey of yours? Something you couldn't tell me about?" He wanted that to be true, but Emily shook her head.

"No, I left because of us. Almost ended my life. Marvelle found me. Told me he had plans for me. Said he saw a halo around me. Certainly didn't believe him at first, but once I saw the child, held her . . . she didn't cry. I felt something grow in my heart that before had been barren. There's some kind of power in her. Marvelle told me she's mine for the raising. Ours, I suppose, since that's what it seems like it's comin' to."

"Does she have a name?" Whistler asked.

"Marvelle never said and I never asked. I just call her

Little One."

"She should have a name."

Emily gazed down at the sleeping child. "If we pick one now it's gotta go with Emily," she said.

"And Henry," Whistler said. His own given name, almost forgotten to the years, rolled thickly off of his tongue. "What names did we have picked out all those years ago?"

"For a girl it was always Dorothy."

Whistler nodded. "It'll still do," he said. "I still like it."

"Dorothy it is then. Feels right naming her with you, starting over like this." Her eyes were brimming with tears. "Henry, there's so many things in the past that I-"

Whistler held up his hand. Dorothy had started stirring and he wanted her to sleep for now. "Let's go to the other room, Em," he whispered. "We've lots to talk about. The past, the future. Got work to do. But at least . . . at least we don't have to be alone anymore. Let's patch our wounds and show this world that we can take whatever it throws at us. Like old times?"

"Like old times," Emily agreed.

Whistler extended his large hand. Emily took it and allowed herself to be led out of Dorothy's room and into the wide, peaceful Kansas farm house.

△▽△▽ • EPILOGUE •▽△▽△

The sound of Whistler's front door slamming open awakened him in the night.

His heart began thundering immediately, sweat coming to his surface. He sat up in bed. "Em," he hissed. "Em." No answer. Whistler had fallen asleep in his clothes and had barely even gotten the blanket over himself. The night was cold and rainy, and his wounds still hurt. His lips, his hand, his leg, his arm. His skin was tight and frigid.

He reached over and slowly grabbed the first thing he could find that would function as a weapon, then he made for the front door, clothes iron gripped tightly in his hand. He hated the thought that things would start up again so soon.

He ran into the front room, determined to meet whatever it was head-on, only to find a man soaking wet and sagging with rain. It wasn't until the man stumbled forward and fell heavily into Whistler's arms that he felt the slippery warmth of blood.

Whistler half dragged, half carried the man over to a chair and sat him gently in it. "You stay here," he said, and he rushed off to grab a candle and some cloth.

"Emily!" Whistler yelled over thunder.

"Hush," she said, coming out of Dorothy's room.

"Thank God you're alright," Whistler said. "We got a visitor." He rummaged through his bureau, trying to find an old shirt that he could sacrifice.

"At this hour?"

"I need your help." Whistler motioned to the chair. He held the candle as Emily attended to the man's wounds. "What's your name?" Whistler asked the man. The man's eyes were closed, his face pained.

"You have the Worldbreaker," he grunted.

"What's your name, man? Who are you?"

"This thing ain't closin'," Emily said, holding rags to the man's arm. "He's gonna bleed to death."

"Where's the nearest doc?" Whistler asked her.

"Twenty miles."

"That ain't good." He turned back to the man. "Where'd you come from? What's a Worldbreaker?" Whistler remembered the angel briefly mentioning that term. He'd dismissed it at the time, now he couldn't.

"She sleeps," the man said. "She sleeps right now, but the storm is coming." His head began to slump. Emily worked frantically to tie off and patch the gash that ran from the man's shoulder to his wrist, but it was a hopeless cause. "Demons," the man whispered.

Whistler's hair bristled anew. "Where? Here?"

"Not anymore," the man said, his face white. "I took – ngh – care of 'em. But they're after her. After the . . . Worldbreaker. This place won't hold 'em off forever. I'm here to tell you, I'm here to tell you . . ."

"Tell us what?"

The man took a bloody hand and started rummaging around in the pocket of his faded green overalls. "You gotta talk to Hook," he said, straining. "I got a map somewhere." He coughed violently. Whistler watched the man's blood pool on the floor. "The demons know too much. Gotta . . . get to Hook."

He died with his hand still in his pocket, not having found whatever he was looking for.

Whistler gently pulled the man's hand out and reached into the pocket. He found a wet piece of paper and unfolded it. The ink was mostly legible.

"What is it?" Emily asked.

"Map," Whistler replied. "You were right, Em. Our journey isn't over." He turned the soggy piece of paper so that his wife could see it. "Looks like we're goin' somewhere."

"We'll talk about this tomorrow," Emily said as thunder boomed. Dorothy started crying. "Ain't nothin' to be done about it tonight I don't think." She closed the dead man's eyes, then went to wash her hands and take care of the baby.

Whistler figured he had business to be about right now, too.

"Just as I feared," he said to the dead man as he hoisted him onto his shoulder. "This ain't over."

And Whistler heard the wind howling outside.

The End of Whistler's Angel
Worldbreaker: Book 1

HISTORICAL FIGURES

Whistler's Angel is a work of fiction, but many of the characters were real people from American history, or literary characters from other works of fiction. I've put this section at the end of the book to shed a little more light on their stories without ruining any twists.

I fictionalized their stories, fudging dates and character attributes to make everything hum, but there is a kernel of truth to each of them. Here is a synopsis of each character.

Whistler ("Uncle" Henry) - Of *The Wizard of Oz* fame. Uncle Henry is not actually Dorothy's uncle, but rather her adoptive parent. The actual relationship is not thoroughly explored in *The Wizard of Oz*, and it was something I had started to wonder about. I thus chose to make Worldbreaker an exploration of where Dorothy Gale came from, and what she actually means to the world. I hope to explore this much further in the next installment.

John Henry - Most of John Henry's story in Whistler's Angel is true - or as close to the truth as history can come. There's still debate on whether John Henry was actually real or not. That uncertainty only increases his legend. John Henry was a slave turned railroad worker whose might was heralded by the men of his day. He eventually was freed and got a job driving spikes into mountainsides to help clear paths for tunnel construction. It is fabled that he won a race against a steel-driving machine, only to pay for the victory with his life when his heart gave out from the strain.

Lillian Smith - Lillian was Annie Oakley's rival in Buffalo Bill's Wild West. She's not as well known as Annie because, despite her massive talent, she had a fiery personality and didn't know how - or was unwilling - to act "proper" in front of foreign dignitaries and influential businessmen. She was also a shameless flirt and a risque dresser. But, despite all of these things, she still represented the greatest rival Annie Oakley ever had, and one of the greatest female sharpshooters in history.

Kate Shelley - Kate did indeed save the passenger load of a train by traversing the flooded prairie to warn the station that the Honey Creek bridge was out. She was young at the time, barely fifteen years old. Because of her heroism, she became the first woman in the United States to have a bridge named after her.

Tom Sawyer - Yes, the old man in the general store is none other than Tom Sawyer, Mark Twain's famous rapscallion creation. He's not mentioned by name, of course, but I hoped that his attributes would be recognizable enough. He alludes to the fact that he, at one point, might have been a Hero like Whistler and his friends.

I'm certain that along the way, Whistler will meet many other legends from fiction and reality alike. Enjoy the ride!

ACKNOWLEDGMENTS

Cover Design by Cathy Sheets

A special Thank You to all my Kickstarter backers that made this project possible:

Alan Mood
Marsha Mood
Beth Kille
Dale Mood
Bryan Early
Jim and Mary Jo Zanton
Megan Kehl
Adam Stapleton
Jen McGrath
Caitlyn Zanton
Jeff Ingebritsen
Anthony Del Ciello
Marcio Saban
Colin Moriarty
Eric Schooff
Andy Kerber

www.michaelmood.com